WHEN LIGHTNING STRIKES

SEDONA VENEZ

WANT FREE SEDONA VENEZ BOOKS?

Sign up for Sedona Venez's Newsletter and receive FREE BOOKS. In addition to the free stories, you will also get special pricing, exclusive previews and news of new releases.

GET A FREE SEDONA VENEZ BOOK!

Join Sedona's mailing list to be the first to know of new releases, free books, special prices and other author giveaways.

https://sedonavenez.com/free-book

❧ I ❧

LIGHTNING

MY EYES DARTED toward the door. *Where is Storm?*

My cousin Storm's tardiness was so out of character that my fingers trembled as I took a large gulp of tequila.

I snorted, thinking about our earlier phone conversation. There was no way in hell she'd actually been serious about me attending this meeting without her. She couldn't be, not after I'd specifically told her the last time I'd been around Detective Prick, I had picked up some weird vibes. His emotional compass was not stable. I would crack under pressure if she weren't here.

Shit! I'm already cracking.

I wasn't proud to admit it, but I was desperate. I needed her.

I frantically tapped out a text message to Storm. *Where in the hell are you? I'm not playing, Storm. Get your ass over here. Now!*

I waited. No response. *What in the hell?*

Reason Orlov, my bestie and lawyer, pursed her lips with displeasure while drumming her well-manicured nails against her desk. "So, Light, let me get this straight. She's not coming to this meeting because she had some emergency?"

Leaning back into the chair, I tried to refocus my mind by absorbing the sleekness of Reason's pristine midtown Manhattan office suite. "The last time I spoke to her, she sounded panicked, and that's not like her."

Reason bent toward me with eyes narrowed, as if she were interrogating me on the witness stand. Her drumming increased.

My lips curled up with distaste. Her loud tapping was like fingernails on a chalkboard.

"Reason, I swear, if you don't stop that, I'm going to fly over this damn desk and fucking cunt-punt you." I was already pissed off with Storm for dodging this meeting. I sure as hell didn't need lawyer extraordinaire pumping me for answers I didn't have.

Reason flashed her canines. "Watch it, Light. I'm not putting up with your mood swings today."

Irrationally, my temper flared as I leaned forward. "I don't give a flying fuck, vampire!"

Reason's hazel eyes narrowed with concern. "What's up with you lately?" She sat back, examining me like a lab rat, drumming again.

I pointedly stared at her fingers. "I'm not fucking kidding," I hissed.

I was out of control. I knew it. Reason knew it. But I couldn't rein it in. I wiped my damp forehead with shaky fingers. My empath symptoms were getting worse, and there wasn't shit I could do about it. What had once worked at controlling my intense migraines and wild mood swings—my large consumption of alcohol—was now failing. I tossed back a glass of tequila, gritting my teeth with frustration.

My symptoms were making me a nervous wreck, and even worse, I had slowly been alienating everyone I loved with my erratic behavior. One minute, I would be bawling my eyes out; the next, I would be dripping with rage. There was no middle ground anymore.

"It's getting worse, isn't it?" Reason's tone softened. "You need help, Light. You can't continue down this path without going completely crazy."

I didn't flinch at her bluntness. I respected it. That was why she was my best friend, and I loved her like a sister. Our bond had been formed from practically growing up together. Her family, a long line of lawyers, had been handling all my family's legal affairs for centuries.

"I'm already there, Reason." I swallowed over the bitterness of being the only Credence born as a sensory empath with the unlucky ability to feel humans' energies and emotions.

"Storm thinks I can handle this meeting without her . . . but look at me." I was sweating, as if I'd just run a marathon. My fingers were shaking like a junkie's. And I was yelling like a deranged cast member from a reality show. "I won't last five minutes in the presence of that detective. He's pure evil." I knew, in a matter of seconds after being exposed to him, I'd be overwhelmed by his energy, taking his feelings and losing mine.

Reason's eyes widened with alarm. "Where is Storm? Is she with Knox?"

"She'd better not be." As much as I was relieved Storm had finally been getting some from Knox Gunner, rock star hotness, now was not the time for being knee deep in sweaty sex. We had major issues concerning a detective with a stick stuck up his ass sideways and the likelihood of me going straitjacket insane.

Storm wasn't just my cousin, best friend, and business partner. She was my sanity check from the daily strain of keeping the barrage of human emotions from sending me to Crazy Land.

I was tired of being a burden. I hated I'd been born with the worst luck of all the members in the Credence family. The constant influx of feelings was overwhelming, with no remedy to prevent them from completely making me insane. My family had tried different methods to help. The only two that worked were dulling my senses with alcohol and Storm soothing me through our bond connection. A few sips of her emotions would put my mind in a neutral, calm state.

Reason glowered. "Detective Burrows requested a meeting with both of you. It's too damn late to cancel without arousing further suspicion." She banged on her desk. "Damn it to hell. I can't believe he actually found information on the dead reporter's laptop linking Credence O. to Celina's death."

I snorted. "You and I know that's total bullshit. Someone is framing us."

Reason arched a brow. "Can you be more specific? Your family has more enemies than friends."

I couldn't dispute her point. Despite my family's wealth, we were considered outsiders among Others—wolf-shifters, vampires, and assorted supernatural beings who blended in, coexisting with humans—because of our fae ancestry.

I leveled her with an irritated stare. "Lacie Gilden. Everyone in the coven knows the Gildens are ruthless."

And it didn't help matters that they were our direct business competitors. Their business would go to great lengths to steal our clients and employees. Lacie was a spiteful, bitter she-wolf who tried everything in her power to ruin our prestigious reputation as Credence Other Corporation. Credence O. was secretly New York's most sought-after Others escort service, providing over-the-top discreetness and exclusivity to our clients. Clients included Other men with a preference for Other women, minus all the drama of unnecessary attachments. Our clients demanded the elite of beautiful Other women as arm candy when they were in town on business.

Reason stared in shock. "This is bad. I can't believe all your contracts are missing. Records documenting which client booked which escort, places, times, agreed-upon service fees . . . all gone!"

My jaw tensed as I thought about all the information that safe had held. Paper documentation was not my preferred method of doing business. But the contracts we had with our clients were arrangements dating back centuries, when paper had ruled and a physically signed document had been the only thing honored—a practice that was a recipe for disaster in the wrong hands.

"I don't understand why Storm isn't here yet," Reason said flatly.

I rubbed my now throbbing forehead. "She'll be here." At least that was what I hoped. I'd been calling her like a stalker and had still gotten no response, which was totally out of character for her.

Reason grabbed my hand, gently rubbing it. "Don't worry. Once she gets here, she'll do that weird fae thing and fix you right up."

"I can't continue using her as my crutch," I responded.

"And you can't continue pretending you're resigned to your fate. You'll find a cure, like Demi's vision predicted."

My mouth flattened at the mention of Demi, the daughter of the Coven High Priestess. Demi was adamant the solution to my empath dilemma was a Bringer of Death. Due to her erratic personality and unreliable gift for foreseeing future events, her predictions almost never made sense.

"I love your optimism, but there's no magic fae wand that's going to save my ass."

Reason suggestively wiggled her eyebrows. "It could be a man."

I rolled my eyes. "That's the last thing I need in my life right now. Besides, I'm on a no-sex lockdown."

In the beginning, it had been hard to give up something I loved—sex—but it had become easier as the months had gone by. I didn't need the drama of a man in my life. I was too complicated, too emotional, and definitely too unstable—red flags that made the possibility of having a long-term relationship simply impossible, red flags that enabled my habit of discarding men like disposable shavers. I loved sex . . . lots of it. And I'd control the who, the when, and the how.

That was probably why one of my ex-lovers had endearingly nicknamed me the Sex Dictator for my insistence on directing every lick, move, or touch. And like I'd told him, I wouldn't have had to if he weren't such a hopeless case in bed. Needless to say, he'd stormed out in a huff, leaving me to finish myself—quite well, I might add.

"Maybe that's what you need right now—someone to take the edge off."

I scoffed. "No offense, but I'm not interested in dating advice from someone who hasn't had sex in years."

She pursed her lips. "I'm not willing to settle."

"What you really mean is you're not willing to settle for getting married to some coldhearted vampire your father picked."

Reason was the black sheep in the family. Her mother was a human, and her father was a vampire. Her birth was a shame to her blueblood family, who would do everything in their power to ostracize her. Her father, a powerful and ruthless man, loved her more than life and would do everything in his power to make her fit into the vampire world. But Reason wanted no part of it, totally ignoring his attempts, much to his embarrassment.

"Exactly. He's so obsessed with marrying off his hybrid-vampire daughter that he's willing to make a pact with the devil. Besides, I don't need a man. I'm happy being single."

I rolled my eyes before saying, "Uh-huh."

I heard Tabitha, Reason's administrative assistant, say in a whiny little bitch voice, "You all can't go in there!"

My head snapped around, and my body quivered with unease as I scooted back into my chair. My unease heightened when my body instantly went on high alert, like a cornered animal. I watched with narrowed eyes as the door slammed open. Storm and Knox burst in, followed by four men. My unease increased tenfold when my eyes were drawn to the only man on earth who could simultaneously make my sex clench with lust and my stomach roll with hatred—Ryker Alfero.

Why in the hell is he here?

His sea-green eyes darted to the empty bottle of tequila

sitting in front of me. He snorted with distaste. "Oh, there she is, my beautiful drunk." He held up two fingers. "How many fingers am I holding up?" he asked mockingly.

I gave him the middle finger. "One! Now fuck off!"

Today, I refused to let him ruffle my feathers like he had at his gala the other night. This was business Light, hyper-composed Light, fashionable, elegant, in-charge Light. I'd deliberately chosen to dress the part by wearing my best designer handiwork, a dainty gray petal-collar blouse, five-inch studded black heels, and black pants.

"Baby, your dirty little mouth is making me hot," he growled.

He sauntered toward me with fire in his eyes. I refused to get up. His gaze locked on me as he trapped me against the chair with his beefy arms.

His lips grazed the shell of my ear when he grumbled, "I would love to see what else your dirty little mouth could do."

With those few words, I shivered as a surge of energy zipped into my body, unlocking something I didn't understand. My brain started functioning with a clarity I hadn't experienced in years—no warring emotions, just calmness.

Good God! This shouldn't be happening, especially not with him.

My heart and pulse raced as panic set in. The power snapped like a rubber band, and the dreaded dark emotions came flooding back with a vengeance. Sweat broke out on my forehead while perspiration trickled between my breasts.

"God, this is going to be a rough fucking ride." My voice was hoarse and ragged.

"I'll do my best to break you in slowly, submissive," he hissed, his voice dripping with raw sex.

He took my hand, gripping it tight when a jolt of electricity ran through both of us. His thumb caressed my hand.

My clit thumped against my panties as an erotic image flashed through my mind—me on all fours and those big hands all over my body while he fucked me from behind. When my tongue snaked out to wet my lips, a soft snarl left Ryker's mouth.

Shit! Shit! Shit! I was in serious trouble.

"Let go." I looked pointedly at our clasped hands.

He squeezed mine hard before releasing it.

"I guess you know each other . . ." Reason trailed off, looking between the two of us with an arched brow.

I made no move to explain. Reason turned a curious gaze to Storm, who shrugged.

Reason suddenly cleared her throat. I glanced guiltily at her. She was staring at Ryker and me with a smile on her face, doing absolutely nothing to dismiss the question in her gaze.

I was beyond exasperated as I looked at Storm. "You're late, cousin!"

"Hey, Light. I apologize for being late," Storm muttered while looking at Knox. "Something kept coming up."

She started to stroll toward me, but Knox pulled her back, pinning her to his side.

I truly wanted to choke her for being late, but damn, the girl looked well fucked . . . and happier than I'd ever seen her.

Knox nipped Storm's neck. "Damn right. I can't help it if my mate makes me rock hard."

Storm slapped his arm. "Cut the shit, Knox."

"Mate?" I raised a brow. "What the hell's going on?"

Casually, Ryker sat at the edge of Reason's desk and stared at me. "He's a wolf-shifter. Keep up, darling," he stated dryly.

I considered him from head to toe and back again to his hard lips that looked like they rarely smiled to the scar across his left eyebrow and over to the snake tattoo on the right side of his neck, which completed the don't-fuck-with-me aura. He looked more like a Viking who should be carrying a bloody sword.

Storm responded with an overly exaggerated, "Surprise!" and jazz hands.

Completely ignoring her, I shook my head with an uncharacteristic serious air. "And who are the three idiots?" I glared at the three hulking men standing by the door, staring at me in slack-jawed shock. "More members of the wild kingdom?"

They were far from beastlike; in fact, all three were handsome, freakishly so. My gaze snapped to Ryker. Those intense green eyes were staring at me in a way that shouldn't have made me want him, but I did.

Ryker growled loud enough that Knox protectively pushed Storm behind him.

"They're my enforcers—Soar, Rip, and Jackal," Ryker said with eyes locked on me, "and, darling, if you call me or my pack animals again, I won't be responsible for the next thing I do to your pretty ass."

I moaned like a porn star. "Like what? Bending me over and giving me a spanking because I've been a bad girl?"

His mouth tightened. I bit back a smile, taking pleasure in ruffling his feathers.

I dug in like the vicious witch I was. "Not that I mind a good spanking, but I would prefer my punishment to come from one of your enforcers. It seems I'm more woman than an alpha like you can handle." I sighed playfully while winking at them.

He looked at the empty bottle of tequila sitting in front of me. "They say you can't judge a book by its cover, but in your case, what you see is exactly what you get. Isn't that right, tequila sunrise?"

My smirk fell. "You ass."

Ryker smiled, a slow lifting of perfect lips to reveal straight, white teeth. "When you play with the big dogs, you might get bitten."

I was ready with my smart comeback when one of his enforcers stepped forward, grabbing my hand.

"I'm Rip," he crowed with teeth sparkling.

His piercing blue eyes stared at me with interest—too much for my liking. There was way too much confidence in his surferguy swagger. He looked like something right out of a fashion magazine.

"Really?" I rolled my eyes, removing my hand from his. "My panties will not be dropping for the likes of you, golden boy."

He upped the wattage of his smile. "I like her."

A throat cleared, and the tightly muscled guy with jet-black hair cropped in a buzz cut pushed away from the door. He smiled, flashing a dimple, as he leisurely but thoroughly studied me. "I'm Jackal." He waved his hand over his shoulder and noted dismissively, "That's Soar."

Soar ran his hand over his short-cropped chestnut hair as his mouth curled downward.

Rip puffed his chest, smiling flirtatiously. "So, Lightning, are you single?"

"Rip." Ryker's voice was harsh.

I laughed at Rip's bold flirting. Through the Other rumor mill, I'd heard about Ryker's new enforcers. They didn't look as deadly as Others had made them out to be, but looks were sometimes deceiving.

I glanced at Ryker, who was glaring at Rip with murder in his eyes.

"Nice to meet you three." I leaned closer to Rip. "And I'm *very* single."

His smile widened as his blue eyes left me and moved to where Ryker was sitting on the edge of the desk.

I quickly looked at Storm. "Where's Noah?"

Noah was Storm's friend and an enforcer for the Alfero pack, the largest and toughest New York wolf-shifter pack.

Rip, Jackal, and Soar looked at Knox with raised brows before loudly clearing their throats.

"Noah decided to take a position in England," Rip responded.

I arched a brow. "That was sudden."

Storm grumbled, "Apparently."

"Rip, move," Ryker snapped.

Blinking innocently, Rip turned to him with a wide smile. "Why? If you're not interested, then—"

Ryker moved from the desk. Rip winked at me before sliding back to take his post by the door. Ryker sat back down and scowled.

"Wow. Okay, that was intense," Storm mused loudly while pointedly looking at Knox's arms.

He released her. She smiled, leaning up to kiss him hard before swaggering over to me. Her eyes narrowed. I knew she could see the frayed emotional walls around my mind—that and the fact that I hadn't slept in days.

She softly kissed me on the cheek. "You okay?"

"Not with Wolfie all up in my face."

Storm looked from me to Ryker and then back to me. Her eyes widened. "Oh, I see."

I rolled my eyes. "No, you don't see because . . . there's nothing to see."

Storm smiled cheekily. "Why don't you take your own advice and submit?"

I gritted my teeth. She was throwing back my advice to her about Knox when I'd encouraged her to give him a chance. Ryker and I were not the same. She knew that. I had issues . . . and from the smug look on Ryker's face, he did, too.

"I'll deal with you in private, Stormy Credence," I hissed.

Storm smiled widely. "I'm not scared."

Knox came up behind Storm, wrapping his arms around her waist. "Come on, baby." He winked at Ryker. "Let the alpha play with his new submissive." He pulled her toward the leather sofa while whispering something in her ear.

My eyes narrowed on Knox. "I did like you, rock star. Now? Not so much."

Reason leaned back, silently watching us as if we were some horrible experiment gone wrong. "I feel like I'm missing something here, and I can't figure out what."

I loudly snapped my fingers. "You, lawyer girl, we're paying out the ass for you to do lawyer stuff. Close your mouth and do your job." I nodded over at Ryker and his enforcers. "Get rid of the wild kingdom, and let's get on with business."

Reason rolled her eyes. "Simmer down, Lightning. My job is

to get you out of trouble; it's not to prevent you from getting into it." She stood, strolling over to Storm. "I'm so happy for you, baby cakes." She tightly hugged Storm and then sternly eyed Knox. "She's one of my best friends . . . next to Grumpy over there." She nodded toward me. "You'd better treat her good, shifter."

Knox solemnly stared back at her. "I will."

Reason cracked a smile. "Good. I might be a hybrid vampire, but I can still kick your ass." She winked at him before sauntering back to her desk.

I crossed my arms. "Are you done kissing his ass?"

She raised her eyebrow before sighing. "Are you trying to test my damn patience?"

"No. I'm trying to get you to do your job," I responded snidely.

Reason stared at me with a frown before the phone on her desk rang. "Yeah? What's up, Tabitha?" she answered, hitting speaker phone.

"Detective Burrows called. He's running late."

"Good, because I'm going to need time to rein in this circus," she responded dryly while looking at me before disconnecting sharply.

"*Oh*, wait, are you actually going to do your job?" I snapped.

Ryker smiled charmingly as he grabbed ahold of my chair, pulling it in so his huge muscled legs straddled mine. "Darling, don't be rude. Adults are talking."

When he suddenly leaned in, putting his nose against my neck, I refused to flinch. His appealing aromatic smell of expensive cigars, sandalwood, and rich earth wafted around me. I almost dropped at his feet. I hated myself for this weakness.

"What is it about the Credence scent that's so alluring?" He took another sniff. "Is it the rare combination of fae and witch blood?"

I rolled my eyes. Others were fascinated by the fact that my family were the last of the fae—mystical Others with the ability to wield great power in magic.

Credence scent? God, he is such an ass.

I bit back the hysterical bubble of laughter at his cocky, sexy smile. I was positive that smile had countless women, Others and humans, melting at his feet. It was like I was some trophy he wanted to mount on his fucking wall. He thought I was some game, and fucking me would be his grand prize. I saw the eerily familiar predatory look in his eyes. It was the same predatory stare I would give to men I was determined to sample to scratch my sexual itch.

I arched a brow at him. *Oh, Wolfie is in for a rude awakening.* I wasn't interested in the bullshit he was selling, and he needed to understand that . . . now.

I brought up my knee, aiming for his nuts, smiling with glee.

Oh, alpha, this is going to hurt . . . a lot.

2

RYKER

My lips quirked. She was luminous with her perfect smile and smooth skin, which shone under a jet-black topknot. But . . . she was too easy to read. I smoothly grabbed her knee. My hand slid around her long leg, pulling it up and out, and then I draped it over my knee, holding her thigh wide open, indecently.

God, this woman is absolutely gorgeous. She was mean yet fucking stunning.

Dammit, I didn't need this shit right now, not with her. She was an abrasive, foul-mouthed hellcat who wreaked havoc on my unshakable, controlled demeanor. No, I definitely didn't need this chaos in my life, not when I had a pack and the Other Council relying on me.

She rolled her eyes with disgust. I pressed my palm to her thigh, firmly restraining her attempt to jerk it away. And in that moment, something happened between us.

I heard a woman's voice . . . Light's voice . . . whisper, *"Oh God, not another Nolan,"* in my mind.

"Who the hell is Nolan?" I growled.

Light's eyes widened with shock before she blankly stared at me. A growl rumbled in my chest. I was pissed she was thinking of another man in my presence. My primal impulse reared its head, and my mind raced with the overwhelming need to shift and take her down like a deer.

Mine.

I hadn't felt this out of control in years.

I possessively dragged a digit along her inner thigh. I could feel the change in her body temperature. Sensuous heat radiated off her in huge waves. Her lips parted, and her fingers crept across the top of my hand before digging in her fingernails. My cock jerked, ramping up my irrational urge to have her. Something about Light made me crazy and damn near feral. This woman had the potential to splinter the ironclad control I had over my beast, self-discipline I had worked years to establish. No, this was dangerous . . . to me and Others. Now was not the time to lose restraint over a woman.

And just like that, our connection shattered.

She shoved me. "Get off me!" she murmured. "I'm not fucking kidding."

I removed my hand. I hadn't wanted to, but I did. I wasn't going to force this.

I leaned back, dropping her leg with a thud. She pursed her lips.

I stared at her mouth with her pretty pouty lips that would look quite lovely around my cock.

Light folded her arms in front of her chest, silently regarding me for several minutes. "Is there a problem, Wolfie?"

"If you call me Wolfie again, there will be."

She smiled icily. "Oh, I'm sorry. Do you prefer Beast Man or Wolf Man or—"

"You could use my name."

She shot me an evil glare. "I could, but that wouldn't be half as fun, would it?"

I smiled nonchalantly when I smelled her anxiety. I casually examined her, taking in her cool demeanor on the outside. On the inside, she was apprehensive around me for some reason, and I was determined to find out why. I leaned forward, grabbing a lock of her long, jet-black hair and wrapping it around my finger.

LIGHT'S EYES DILATED. "FIRST, DON'T TOUCH ME. SECOND, don't touch me."

My eyes narrowed on the hair I had around my forefinger, my thumb rubbing it against my skin. I marveled at how beautiful she was with her soft skin, long hair framing her gorgeous face, and the sexiest, tightest curvy body I'd ever seen. I heard her sharp intake of breath and the increase of her heartrate.

She jerked her head. I tightened my grip. Her eyes narrowed.

I could see the wheels turning in her head, debating on whether to tug her head and risk losing a couple of strands in the process.

"Let go, Wolfie," she ground out. "I don't like to be touched."

I knew I should let her go, but I'd never met a woman who simultaneously made me hard and angry. She yanked her head. I quickly let go, moving nearer. She slammed back against the chair, desperately trying to avoid contact. The chair teetered. I smiled devilishly, slanting in closer. She leaned even farther away.

Her eyes sharpened as the chair wobbled back, heading for a painful crash to the floor. "Motherfuck—"

I grabbed the chair, righting it with a thump. "You all right, darling?"

Light shoved me. I didn't budge. She gritted her teeth in frustration.

I slowly moved away, proving my point. She wasn't in control. I was.

Her eyes glittered with anger. "Idiot." She started to stand.

I grasped her chair, pulling it in so close that my legs straddled hers again.

She cleared her throat, trying to maintain a bit of calm. "Get the hell off me." She brushed her hair away from her face. "I'm. Not. Interested."

Her emotions were so strong I could almost see as well as feel them. And she wanted me.

I bit my inner cheek to stop my grin. "Are you sure about that? Because I smell interest all over you, darling."

Light smiled evilly as she stared over at Reason's desk. I glanced over my shoulder and saw Reason snatching her silver letter opener from the top of her desk.

"Oh, hell no! You are not stabbing him with the opener. I don't want bloodstains all over my new furniture. I just had my office redecorated," Reason snapped.

"Right here, darling." I brushed a finger across Light's neck, taking satisfaction when she shivered deliciously. "Don't get distracted by bright, shiny things."

"And what the hell is up with all the touching?" She leveled me with a murderous glare. "I'm not fucking kidding. Move!"

"As you wish." I drew away, deliberately grazing the side of her breast with my hand.

She hissed with pursed lips.

"What's wrong, darling?" I asked dryly. "You seem . . ." I traced a finger across her cheek.

She swatted my digit. "Annoyed?"

When I smelled panic washing over her like waves, I almost felt sorry for her—*almost*—but something about Light stoked the flames of my sadistic streak. And I wanted Lightning Credence to squirm.

My face dissolved into a delicious grin. "Panicked."

Light gripped the chair's armrest. "I am—"

I deliberately cut her off while wrapping a strand of her hair around my finger. "Exactly."

"I am not panicked," she finished while pointedly eyeing me.

"That's not what I smell right now."

She gave me an incredulous stare.

"You're on the verge of running out of here with your tail between your lovely legs." I mockingly stared at her. "And I can give you a much more pleasurable preview of the things I'm going to do once I get between them . . ."

She stiffened.

"Relax. Your secret is safe with me, darling." I winked.

She rolled her eyes. "What secret?"

"That you regret turning down my offer to give you the best fuck you've ever had."

Light scowled. "I doubt you have the ability, Wolfie, to handle a woman like me."

I dragged a digit across her cheek. "Oh, darling, I can't wait to disprove your theory." I smiled, enjoying watching her squirm. "You know the offer still stands. And I won't even make you beg . . . much." Making her beg had been the only thing on my mind since our run-in at my charity gala.

3

RYKER

A COUPLE NIGHTS PRIOR...

I stormed into my ornately furnished office while glancing down at my watch. Knox and Rip brought up the rear, making sure no one followed before the door closed. Beautiful antiques glinted in the moonlight coming in through the French doors and over Calum, the leader of the most powerful pride of tiger-shifters in New York.

"Bearer of the Sword of Souls," Calum calmly greeted me, "nice of you to finally grace me with your presence." He stood facing the French doors, with his hands clasped behind his back.

I strode in the middle of the room where Bones, Soar, and Jackal were already standing tensely in a faceoff with Calum's enforcers.

"Is there a reason you wanted to meet with me?" I barked. "In case you didn't realize, I have a charity gala going on right now."

"When you became leader of the Other Council, you pledged to unite the Others and bring peace to New York. Your pledge was the only reason I agreed to a truce with the Others." Calum turned to face me. His eyes were yellow, and his body was tense. "Does our truce still hold, wolf-shifter?"

I bristled at his question. "It holds for as long as I say it does."

"Then tell me why the bodies of two of my top enforcers were found dumped in the middle of Manhattan with their hearts ripped out," Calum stated with barely concealed rage. Tiger-shifters were solitary beasts that liked to spend most of their time alone, roaming their massive territories, looking for food. But Calum managed to rally a small contingent of tiger-shifters under his strong leadership.

My eyes narrowed on Calum as Soar, Rip, Jackal, Knox, and Bones flanked me. "And you're assuming this is the handiwork of wolf-shifters?"

Calum gazed at me, appalled. "This is fact. The smell of wolf-shifters was all over the bodies."

"No wolf would have done that unless I'd sanctioned it," I snarled.

Calum coolly stared at me. "That's exactly what I thought, so I'll ask again. Does the truce between the Others still stand?"

I growled as the painful tingle of the feral power of the Sword of Souls coursed through my fingers. I clenched my palms, fighting the appearance of the Sword into my hand. I watched everyone in the room involuntarily bare their necks. Everyone felt my tension and waited anxiously for my next move.

Calum snarled. His canines dropped. "So now you've chosen to abuse your power as the wielder of the Sword?"

I slowly closed my eyes and blew out a cleansing breath, aware that my power was rolling off me. My eyes flew open. The power snapped like a rubber band. "Someone has decided to wage war with my pack by killing your enforcers, thereby breaking the truce. Rest assured, I will find out who's behind this."

Calum adjusted his tuxedo. "Ensure that you do, wolf. Our truce will not hold unless you get this under control."

He nodded to his enforcers. They all paraded out of the office without a second glance.

I was pissed at Calum's accusation. I already had my hands full when the goddess of death had appointed me the leader of the Other Council, promising the shifters—tigers, lions, wolves, dragons, and bears—a new beginning. The new beginning would include cleaning up years of shifter wars, started by my out-of-control father.

I pinched the bridge of my nose and blew out a deep breath. Whoever decided to kill those shifters had knowingly declared war on my pack. It was time to show my enemies that I had no qualms about removing the threat. No one disrespected my authority and survived.

Knox frowned, gazing at me. "You all right?"

"As good as I'm going to be," I responded tiredly. "Two tiger-shifters killed during a fragile truce is not exactly good news."

Knox stared at me and then back to the others. "There is no way the negotiation for a permanent Others peace pact will happen until this gets resolved."

I grimaced at Knox, my younger brother and recently appointed beta wolf, the second-in-command. I was proud of Knox but wondered if thrusting him into power so fast was smart. Living as Knox Gunner the rock star was one thing, but being second-in-command of a pack of shifters was a lot of responsibility, especially for a pack that was in the rebuilding stage.

I frowned. It wasn't just Knox who had a lot to learn about navigating the choppy waters of Others society. I had been estranged from Others society for so many years, so some days, I'd wonder if all the powers shoved upon me were too much, too soon. My jaw tightened, and I quickly dashed away the self-doubt.

The goddess of death never made mistakes. She had chosen me for a reason. I was the only one she trusted to bring the Others back from the brink of annihilation. It was my obligation to right all the wrongs my bloodline had done to create dissension among the Others. I knew it wouldn't be easy, but I was making headway. With the help of Knox and my friends—Rip, Jackal, and Soar—I was determined to rebuild trust. But first, the Others must understand my word was law.

I leveled my pack with a hard stare. "We need to find out who killed those shifters. I need everyone to reach out to their contacts. I want solid intel by the end of the night."

The heavy pounding of the music strummed annoyingly, reminding me that the charity gala was still in full swing. I truly hated these events, but socializing with Others on occasion was a necessary evil. I had to lead by example, showing coven, pride, and pack leaders that we could coexist in peace.

At the urging of my Aunt Rosa, I'd organized a series of charitable events with a freaky, sensual twist for Others who indulged in kinky escapades. To my surprise, my events had grown to be one of the hottest invites in the human and Others social circles, and invites were sent to only my wealthy associates who were more than willing to give generously to my charitable foundation.

I smoothed the sleeves of my black tux. "Let's get this gala wrapped up. We have more pressing business to attend to."

We all exited the office and went back into the gala, which was in full swing. The high-octane mixture of new money and old money permeated the room. I ignored the stares and whispers of the glittering women and cigar-smoking men as I strolled menacingly through the crowd of Others—shifters, vampires, and human nobility.

A waiter shuffled over, presenting me with a glass of scotch. Others nodded respectfully, shocked that I'd turned up for my own event. Nine times out of ten, I wouldn't, but tonight, something had been stirring within my beast, urging me to attend.

Sophie, a thin blonde dressed in a skintight red gown, strolled up to me, smiling seductively.

"Sophie, you look beautiful, as always." I stopped, admiring her long legs.

Sophie Jenson was one of the most sought-after actresses in Hollywood. She was also an alpha female wolf-shifter who was strong, smart, and cunning, much desired traits within the circle of wolf-shifter alphas.

She smirked, fully appreciating how I looked dressed up for my charity gala. She reached up to kiss me on the lips. I politely leaned away, chastely kissing her on the cheek. Her eyes hardened and her grin slipped before she tilted her lips into a forced smile.

"All for you." She laid her fingers on my cheek, but I pulled away.

I knew what she wanted—to become my mate and alpha female of my pack. But she was like a sister to me, and we were never going to work as a couple, something Sophie refused to accept.

Taking a deep breath, I turned to my pack. "I'll meet you in five minutes."

Knox, Bones, Jackal, Soar, and Rip regarded each other before stealing a glance at Sophie. I knew exactly what they were thinking. Sophie was trouble with a capital T.

Sophie was the daughter of Harvey Jenson, alpha of the Jenson pack, the second strongest pack in New York, after mine. Harvey and Ryker's father had been childhood friends and had forged an alliance years ago, hoping their children would one day unite their packs through our mating. That was not even a remote possibility as far as I was concerned, and that was even before I'd decided to leave the pack at eighteen to make my own way, not wanting anything to do with the forced mating or the power-mad man my father had become.

When I'd returned to claim my position as alpha, I'd fucked Sophie once, a mistake I had been paying for ever since. That one night had motivated her to ramp up her one-woman campaign to press for an alliance and mating between us. She refused to take the hint that I wasn't looking for a mate.

"There is nothing between us and never will be. You can't keep doing this," I remarked coolly.

A woman strolled past me, leering at me with interest.

Human. I glanced away. I hadn't slept with a human since college. They were way too clingy and wanted commitment. I wasn't a one-woman man . . . and forever wasn't in my vocabulary.

"Doing what? This?" Sophie shot me a bewitching grin, reaching down between my legs to wrap her fingers around my shaft.

In a flash, I grabbed her wrist, bringing it against my chest. "Yes, that." I sighed heavily. "Sophie, you need to find a nice mate to settle down with."

I felt the hostile stare from across the room. Jacob, a wolf-shifter who worked for her father, had been actively pursuing her for months.

"Like Jacob." I released her wrist.

"Jacob?" Sophie flushed. "Are you serious? I don't want Jacob. I want you."

That was the other thing that turned me completely off from Sophie. She was a spoiled brat who viewed things and people as her possessions.

"Want? I'm not your possession."

She planted her hands on her hips. "When you turned your back on your pack to find yourself, I waited. When you came back and beat your uncle for the alpha position, I waited. When the members of your pack deserted you, I waited." Her eyes narrowed. "But I'm done waiting. You need a strong mate to keep the pack together, a mate with powerful pack ties. I can help you rebuild." Her eyes were cold and calculating. "I know you will never love me. Frankly, I don't give a shit about love."

I smiled coldly. "And your gracious offer has absolutely

nothing to do with the fact that your father is ill and my uncle is poised to take over your pack as alpha?"

She flinched like I'd physically slapped her.

"Or the fact that he wants you as his mate?"

She sniffed with disdain. "I will do what is best for my pack. But obviously, I would like to explore other options."

I was the other option. I didn't blame her. She was desperate to save her father's pack from being taken over by Peter, my uncle.

Peter was crazy, ruthless, and consumed by the need for power. He was so consumed that he'd killed my father and appointed himself alpha of the Alfero pack. In the blink of an eye, gone was the life I had built within the human world. The goddess of death had ordered me to reclaim my bloodline, forcing me to go back to the world I had turned my back on and fight Peter for the position of alpha.

I rubbed the scar across my brow, one of the many reminders of that hard-fought battle.

I gritted my teeth. "I'm not going to mate with you, Sophie, but I assure you my uncle will not become alpha of your pack."

"My father and the elders"—her voice broke before she cleared her throat—"think you must take me as your mate to unite our packs, preventing a shifter war."

Narrowing my eyes on Sophie, I growled, "I don't give a shit what they think."

"God, I'm sorry I even brought this up." She bowed her head, not meeting my eyes. "There are whispers among the Others that, without a strong mate, your position as alpha will be in danger."

I knew she wasn't sorry at all.

Despite the fact that my pack was smaller in number, we were still a force to be reckoned with. My pure bloodline ensured that, but as the bearer of the Sword of Souls, wielder of life and death, it pretty much sealed my fate and service to the goddess of death for the rest of my life. No one could kill me, for I was the epitome of death and destruction.

Power surged through my veins. "You go back and tell your father, elders, and my uncle that if they want to challenge me, they'd better be ready, because I will show them no mercy." I paused. "And as far as you and I go, there is nothing between us. Never was; never will be. Now, run along."

Sophie stiffened, standing a bit straighter. "You will need me, Ryker . . . very soon." She bitterly smiled at me before marching away in a huff.

I bristled, knowing Sophie and her father would not give up until they found a way to get what they wanted—me mated to her—creating an alliance they had waited years to happen.

I gulped my glass of fifteen-year-old scotch.

My fucking night had been completely ruined—first, by finding out two shifters had been killed in my territory, and now, by Sophie. I nodded toward Soar, indicating I was done for the night and leaving, when a familiar scent hit me.

Lightning Credence.

I turned casually, examining as she swayed right past me and through the crowd, sipping a glass of champagne. With utter disdain, she ignored the appreciative stares of men. I observed as someone caught her eye—Lacie Gilden, a wolf-shifter and owner of an Others escort company. Light stared boldly at Lacie's date, a bear-shifter, giving him a sexy smile, which made the shifter stop midsentence, checking her out in typical shifter fashion. Light's eyebrow arched with a look in her eyes that I knew all too well, a look I used on many women. It was a look that said, *Once you fuck me, you won't remember your name.*

The bear-shifter swallowed hard. Light laughed at the expression on his face before turning on her heel and strutting through the party.

My cock jerked. *Holy hell, what a fucking strut.* It was sensuous, like a stripper. I had seen her at a couple of events, and though she was captivatingly beautiful, she wasn't my type. I liked my women demure and submissive. From what I'd heard about her erratic party-girl lifestyle, Lightning Credence was a pit bull in a dress. Yet something about her scent pulled on my cock like a leash, commanding me to stop and pay attention.

I watched her flag down a waiter.

"Do you have anything stronger than this?" she drawled, holding up her empty glass.

"Scotch," the waiter replied.

"I hate scotch," she grumbled. "With the amount of money floating around this place, would it have killed Mr. Alfero to have an open bar?"

God, she was beautiful . . . stunning, if she wasn't half drunk.

I silently took several long steps toward her while she appraised the guests.

I slid behind her. "What is that supposed to mean?" I murmured.

She turned, slamming right into my chest. Her eyes widened at the sight of me.

I continued. "Champagne not strong enough for Lightning Credence?"

Her almond-shaped hazel eyes blinked rapidly. I heard her heart race as she pulled her long jet-black hair away from her neck. The image of her hair gliding across my body as she slipped her head between my thighs flashed through my head.

What. The. Fuck?

I usually had more control of myself than this, but her alluring essence slammed against me, rendering me speechless for a moment.

I forced myself to speak. "Darling," I uttered, "are you all right?"

She let out a shaky breath. "Uh . . ." Her back straightened as she smoothed out her skintight cream lace gown.

I took a sip of my drink. "I'm Ryker—"

"Alfero," she snapped.

She'd cut me off. This was new. Women never cut me off.

She continued. "Alpha of one of the largest and most powerful wolf-shifter packs in New York and leader of the Other Council." She looked me up and down. "You don't look as feral as rumors say." Her eyes narrowed. "Shit, I was expecting you to be foaming at the mouth." She smiled seductively. "Not bad-looking at all . . . if I were into the crazy Viking look."

I stared at her carnal full lips. God, I could imagine all the sinful things those lips were capable of doing. "Thanks, I think." *Christ, I want her.*

I watched her gorgeous lips curl up into a sly smile before she snapped, "It's a compliment, alpha. Not an invitation to fuck."

Oh yeah, I wanted her more and more every second.

Light's eyes squinted at my silence. She raised a brow. "What the fuck's wrong with you? You're staring."

Shit, I loved her voice. It was low and husky, like a lover's touch.

"I'm the silent but deadly type, darling. I let my actions speak volumes . . . in and out of bed."

I couldn't help but notice our discussion was low and oddly sensual in the middle of the packed party.

She sighed. "Idiot wolf-shifters," she muttered under her breath.

She grabbed another glass of champagne from the passing waiter and hurriedly drained it before slapping the empty glass into another waiter's hand. Then she grabbed another glass from the tray before greedily sipping it like water.

I arched a brow. "Should I send out for more alcohol for my beautiful drunk?"

Her eyes blazed as she drained the glass. "Was that your attempt at a joke?"

"It's a fucking point. Slow the hell down. Shit, at the pace you're going, there won't be much left for the rest of my guests." I looked her up and down. "And for the record, tipsy is tolerated, but flat-out drunk is fucking distasteful."

Her unfocused gaze fluttered and then zeroed in on me with

utter disdain "Tolerated and distasteful? Wow! I didn't know wolf-shifters could string together such intelligent words in one sentence. I thought you guys grunted and pointed like cavemen."

My smile slipped. She was trouble. I didn't like or need trouble, not now that I was on the brink of another Others war.

She tauntingly licked the rim of the glass, and my cock jerked. But for one night of hot, uncomplicated sex with the Holy Grail—a member of the Credence bloodline—I could make an exception.

She shooed me with her hand. "Now move along, Wolfie. You're scaring away all the hot bachelors."

I shifted, trying to ease my now rock-hard cock.

She glared at me. "What?"

My cock jerked. I loved how annoyed she sounded. "Just looking at you."

"Don't." The tip of her pink tongue ran across her pouty lips.

I knew I should back away. I had more important things to think about, but shit, her scent was driving me insane. It was a mixture of fae, witch, and something else. Her scent made me so hard that I wanted to bend her over in the middle of the crowd and fuck her so hard she wouldn't remember her name. My beast seconded that sentiment by rattling his cage, fighting me for control, fighting me to get ahold of Light.

"Why?" I responded.

Her eyes shrewdly looked me over. "Because I'm more woman than you can handle, Alfero."

The image of her kneeling at my feet flashed through my head, making me even harder. "Is that a fact?"

"Yes, it's a fucking fact," she snapped.

"You have no clue about the things I can handle"—I stepped closer, watching her gaze travel over my body—"or do handle, given the right motivation."

The arousing scent of interest wafted from her. Unlike most Others, she had strong, clean emotions—anger, anxiety, and now . . . arousal.

She peered at me for a full minute before responding, "I'm not interested."

I frowned. My body tensed. "Excuse me?"

"You heard me. I'm not interested in being another notch on your bedpost with a gold star next to it for actually banging a Credence."

I was shocked. For the first time in a long time, a woman shocked me.

"Are you serious?"

"Deadly." She tilted her head back to see me clearly. "Granted, there's something about you. Something"—she inspected me like she could see deep into my soul, and my caged wolf strutted around like a show dog whining for attention —"wild about you that's mildly intriguing."

Yes. I'd take intriguing if it would get her in my bed. "Intriguing is good," I responded huskily.

"Intriguing is not good. I'm intrigued when I watch models prance up the runway in Milan, but it doesn't mean I want to fuck them." She laughed loudly. "God, what is it about Credence women that makes men so desperate to fuck us? Frankly, it's damn annoying."

She coyly tapped my cheek. "Playtime is over. Now get to stepping, Alfero. Go find yourself some submissive she-wolf you can sell your alpha bullshit to." She smiled widely, toying with me. "You know, a woman stupid enough to settle for less than you're willing to give, whose heart you can break without giving a shit. This woman is off-limits."

She stepped back, but I couldn't stop looking at her. I'd never wanted anyone more in my life. I wanted to fuck her until she screamed . . . and I could tell she was one hell of a screamer.

"Light?"

She appraised me, enjoying herself, like a cat with a mouse. "Ryker?" she mimicked.

I stepped closer and was impressed when she hadn't flinched or backed away. I slid my hand behind her neck, leaning down so our faces were close. "You will be mine." I knew she wanted me. I could smell it all over her like perfume.

Light pulled her head back, looking me in the eyes. "That's not going to happen, Wolfie." She smiled, not a forced one. "Have a good life, Mr. Alfero."

She gave me one last glance before strutting away. I watched her go, my eyes trained on her full, swaying ass.

"You can run, but you can't hide, darling," I hissed, mildly pissed off that my cock was still rock hard from her lingering scent.

Jackal ambled up to me with eyes also trained on Light's ass. "Damn, look at that filly go."

"Back off," I growled. "This one is all mine."

And when I did fuck her senseless and she could no longer remember her name, we both would move on, and I'd go back to concentrating on rebuilding my pack and uniting the Others. But for now, Lightning Credence was mission critical.

$$\text{❁} \quad 4 \quad \text{❁}$$

LIGHTNING

PRESENT TIME...

Shit! It couldn't be normal to dislike Ryker and want him all at the same time. The problem was he was exactly my type—the type of man I wouldn't mind going a few hot, sweaty rounds with, a man who was only interested in one night of rough-and-tumble sex with no commitment. Dammit, he was my version of nirvana, with absolutely no possibility of him hanging around like some pathetic puppy dog after I was done with him.

I moaned but cleared my throat when I saw Reason with her chin propped, regarding me with rapt attention. Damn hybrid was enjoying seeing Ryker infuriate the shit out of me. I almost moaned again when he cockily eyed me with those smoldering sea-green eyes that made my sex clench. Shit, he made me feel like I hadn't had sex in years, not months.

This couldn't be fucking happening. *Why did he have to come along when I am on a no-sex lockdown?*

I was happy with my newfound sex hiatus. It had given me plenty of time to think and learn about myself. Frankly, some of the things weren't pretty, but I was a realist. I was a fucking mess, a mess I'd created by picking all the wrong men—intentionally. Nolan . . . well, he was a prime example of my ability to pick a worthless sack of shit without even trying.

How in the hell did Ryker know I was thinking about Nolan?

Ryker kept examining me. My stomach tightened as heat crawled through my body.

"What?" I snapped.

"I can't figure out why my presence exasperates you so much," Ryker grunted in a smooth, deep voice.

"Can I ask you a question?" I whispered sweetly.

"Shoot, darling."

"Why are you here? You don't care about my family, so you aren't here for justice. You don't care about Celina's death, so you aren't here because you're outraged on behalf of the shifter community. And you damn sure don't care about the death of the reporter. So what is it, Ryker? Are you here to irritate me because I rebuffed you?"

He blankly watched at me. "Nope. I'm waiting."

Reason leaned back in her chair. "Waiting? Look, Mr. Alfero . . ."

He coolly gazed at Reason. "You can call me Ryker."

Reason returned his nonchalant stare. "Okay, Ryker. Now, as much as I love watching the foreplay between you and Light, this situation has nothing to do with you or the Other Council. This is a Credence family issue. So I agree with Light. Why are you here?"

I caught sight of the vein along his jaw pulsing—the only tell-tale sign of how bothered he was by Reason's question.

Knox stared at Ryker. "Ryker, tell them."

Ryker glared at him. "Having a brother is starting to be a big pain in the ass," he growled.

Knox looked intently right back at him.

"Fine. Three shifters have been found dead in the span of a couple of days," Ryker said.

Bullshit! He was hiding something else. I snorted. "So this has absolutely nothing to do with the war brewing between the

Others?" I pursed my lips. "Or the temporary truce? Because it seems like a bad time for the city of Manhattan to be raining shifter bodies."

"I'm impressed. Didn't think a party girl like you gave a shit about Others business," Ryker jeered.

My body stiffened. *Is this prick actually insinuating I am too shallow to care about Others?* "You would be surprised at the amount of information a *party girl* like me knows, Wolfie," I spit. "Like how the temporary truce is bullshit. It has to be, or bodies wouldn't be piling up all under your watch . . . alpha."

Soar sharply looked at me. "Watch yourself, fae witch."

Ryker cut him off, coldly looking at me. "A few bodies are a drop of water in the bucket compared to the amount of death that would be happening right now if I hadn't fought for the *bullshit* truce you think ain't worth shit." His jaw tensed. "I'm the only thing standing in the way of a fucking full-scale Others war. So you think about that shit while you're sleeping nice and safe in your luxury home, darling."

My mouth tightened. "Are you expecting some damn gold star for cleaning up the chaos your father created under his reign as alpha?" I paused, annoyed and disappointed in him. "Others don't need your fucking diplomacy. They need your unleashed power."

His eyes flashed, his feral power rolling off him, but he quickly reined it in. Just like that, I knew he was a lethal wolf. He was a fucking ticking time bomb, waiting to explode. God, the man's control seemed . . . too forced. That was the exact reason Others were wary of him, especially since the goddess of death had appointed him as the bearer of the Sword of Souls, with the full power and authority to take or give life. No one wanted to cross him, so they would nod and agree to his demands in front of his face and scoff at his authority behind his back.

I blew out a calming breath before continuing. "I'm not trying to belittle your authority." Honestly, I wasn't. "The Others only agreed to the temporary truce to appease you. You and I know the war and killing between Others never stopped." This was the truth, the elephant in the room no one wanted to acknowledge. "It's like Others forgot our history—a history that included the few humans who knew of our existence hunting us like animals and Others hunting humans in retaliation." I finished.

Reason arched her brow. "As much as I hate to admit it, Light's right. Others kill each other off all the time. Why are these three deaths so important?"

"Because four bodies with their hearts ripped out is too ritualistic," Ryker stated.

"Four? You said three," I declared.

He sharply glanced over at Reason. "Three shifters and one vampire . . . Dimitri."

Reason's eyes widened. "Dimitri? As in my father's second-in-command?"

He nodded.

"This is not good," Reason responded while fumbling with her cell. She marched over to the corner of the room, saying into the phone, "Let me speak to Dad."

My mouth went dry. This most certainly was not good. Reason's father, Oskar Orlov, the leader of the New York vampire coven, was protective of his coven. He was ruthless and, frankly, a little bizarre, but he kept his vampires on a tight leash. To kill one of his own, especially his second-in-command, was like declaring war on Oskar, and no one was stupid or crazy enough to do that.

"The shifters—who were they?" Storm replied sharply.

Ryker crossed his beefy arms. "Two top enforcers from the Calum pride and Houston, Harvey Jenson's beta."

My eyes widened. Calum was the leader of the most powerful pride of tiger-shifters in New York, and Harvey Jenson was alpha of the Jenson pack of wolf-shifters. I stood up, looking worriedly at Storm, who was already walking back and forth. She stopped, and our eyes locked.

"All four of them were our clients," I whispered.

Storm calmly looked at me. "Okay, wait. This could all be some weird coincidence."

"Coincidence? No way in hell. First, Celina was found dead —" I stated.

Jackal interrupted. "She was killed. My sources say she was burned alive in her vehicle."

"Oh God! Burned alive?" Storm eyed Jackal.

I felt like the walls were closing in on us. "First Celina, then the reporter, and now . . ." I swallowed nervously. "Four clients?" I looked over at Reason and recognized the panicked look in her eyes. "I need a fucking drink. When our mothers find out, they're going to kill us."

Storm pointed at me. "No drinking. I need your ass coherent." She tapped her foot. "This has to be tied to the break-in at our office. Our stolen client list is at the center of this debacle. I know it."

"You think?" I spit sarcastically.

"Well, it's official. The avalanche of shit continues." Reason slammed her cell onto her desk. "My father has been locked away in an emergency coven meeting for hours. That's not good." She looked at Ryker. "The coven is ready to pull out of talks to sign the permanent Others peace treaty."

"What peace treaty?" Storm and I inquired in unison.

Soar glared at them. "For those of you who have your heads stuck under rocks, the truce was only a verbal agreement. A permanent peace treaty will make the truce binding."

"Why are you speaking to us like we're two-year-olds?" Storm snapped.

I rubbed my head as the migraine came back full force. "I am so close to losing it right now." I watched Soar. "Why don't you punch yourself in the face so I don't have to do it myself?"

I saw the look in Storm's eyes. She was just as pissed off with

Soar. Storm and I were very aware of Others history and politics, including the backgrounds of each member of Ryker's pack.

"We"—Storm gestured over to me—"always do our fucking research." She paused. "When Ryker became leader of the Other Council, we know he also pledged to unite the Others and bring peace to New York."

I strolled over to Soar. "We also know the only reason the tiger-shifters and vampires agreed to end the killing, via a temporary truce, was if Ryker kept the wolf-shifters on a tight doggy leash."

I'd made it my business to watch Others' antics. It was more entertaining than a reality show. Plus, there was a lot more blood and sex involved. I knew more about Others politics and society gossip than most people suspected. Shit, I'd watch Others politics and society like an MMA fight, except Others were more ruthless.

Soar looked at me with ice-cold eyes. "There's a whole lot you don't know, hybrid."

I smiled frigidly. Oh, the wolf-shifter didn't like me for some reason. Now he was trying to make some sort of an example of me. It was time to teach him a fucking lesson. *Thou shall not fuck with my family or me.*

I stared at Jackal. "You, Jack Alagona, are interesting."

Jackal shot me a genuine smile. "That's what the ladies tell me."

I continued. "You come from a middle-class family who couldn't afford to send you to college, which was the only reason you joined the military—to pay for college. And your expertise in the military was hand-to-hand combat."

"I'm impressed, sweetness," Jackal responded.

Rip groaned. "Smart and beautiful. Now why in the world didn't I meet you sooner?" he commented with a huge smile on his face.

I winked at him. "I'm a lot of woman, Restin Peace—maybe too much woman for you."

He glanced over at Ryker and then looked back at me. "Too bad you're already spoken for, because I sure as hell would love to find out."

I smiled at him. He was a sexy teddy bear. "You, Restin, are a flirt. And you're also the son of a billionaire oil tycoon who was not happy when you dropped out of an Ivy League college to join the army. You're a weapons expert and recently retired from the military." I winked at him. "And according to gossip, you're also what I call a man-whore—a cute one, but a man-whore nonetheless."

"True, but I can be converted by the right woman," Rip responded.

"Is the fucking I Love Lightning tribute over?" Soar snarled.

I arched a brow. "And you, Adam Soar, came from a poor family who, unfortunately, was killed by a coven of vampires. You're ex-military, and your expertise is explosives." I pursed my lips. "You also seem to have a big fucking chip on your shoulder because of how poor you grew up."

Soar scoffed. "You don't know shit about me."

I stepped closer, ready to kick his nuts up into his throat. "Don't make me drop you to your knees, wolf-shifter." I leaned over the desk, making sure to brush Ryker's arm, and picked up the heavy letter opener.

"Make your move, princess," Soar mocked.

"I really wouldn't go there, Soar," Reason mumbled.

I wanted to laugh at the condescending look on Soar's face. Others always underestimated me. That was a tragic mistake, because if there was one thing every Credence woman learned, it was how to defend herself—and not with bullshit aerobic kickboxing. No, we learned to maim and kill. We had to. Others killed and hunted for sport, and the Credence family was hated by Others because, in their eyes, fae witch hybrids were an abomination.

While Storm had learned how to fight and defend herself via lessons with Noah, I had hung out in Brooklyn with a rough, scrappy group of wolf-shifters who embraced me as their own. The leader, my former boyfriend, was an underground street fighter who had taught me how to fight dirty.

Soar laughed, but his laugh quickly died when he saw the chilliness in my eyes. I smiled disdainfully as I threw the letter opener within inches of his head.

Soar jumped back. "You crazy—"

"That skill was taught to me courtesy of my first boyfriend, an underground street fighter." I winked at Ryker. "He also taught me how to master the art of giving enjoyable blow jobs." I rolled my eyes with delight. "Lots of hot, sweaty lessons, but I eventually got the hang of it."

Ryker gave me a panty-dropping smile. "Let me be the judge of that, darling."

Storm cleared her throat. "Okay, all of this is amusing, but let's get back to the peace pact."

Ryker sighed heavily. "This information cannot leave this room."

We nodded.

He continued. "I'm trying to negotiate a peace pact between the tiger-shifters, vampires, and wolf-shifters. Our first serious meeting was scheduled to take place this week. Now, with the recent killings, that shit will never happen."

"An official peace pact would be a game changer," I responded.

"Exactly, and I need to get the talks back on track," Ryker snapped.

The intercom handset rang. "Yes?" Reason spoke into the phone.

"There's a Detective Burrows here to see you," Tabitha replied crisply.

Reason sighed and then commented into the phone, "Give me five minutes, and then send him in."

I swallowed hard. I didn't have a good feeling about this. Storm worriedly regarded me while whispering something to

Knox. She glided over and reclined on the sofa opposite where he was sitting.

She patted the spot next to her. "Light, get your ass over here. I don't want you getting us in any trouble," she jokingly sang. But she and I both knew I was seconds away from snapping like a twig.

"You okay?" Ryker inquired.

"I'm fine." I blew out a breath before striding over to sit by Storm as calmly as I could muster.

Reason's eyebrows knitted while staring at us. "*O-kay*. You two, don't do that double-teaming thing you do. We don't want to aggravate Burrows. We want this to be short and to the point." She deliberately looked at me. "Light, please don't get defensive. I know this is going to be tough, given the situation." She paused, straightening her jacket. "All right, let's put on a show to beat all shows."

We heard a brief knock before Detective Burrows entered the office. Immediately, I was bombarded with his warped, sadistic emotions, emotions that made me sick to my stomach. He stopped short upon seeing Ryker and his enforcers. He glared at Reason.

"Detective, I believe you've met Stormy and Lightning Credence," Reason declared.

We both nodded.

Soar sharply shut the door.

Burrows's mouth tightened while he looked around with narrowed eyes. "What's going on here?"

She gestured toward Ryker. "This is Mr. Alfero and his business associates."

"I know who Mr. Alfero is. What is he doing here?"

Ryker silently looked at him.

"I wasn't expecting . . ." Burrows sputtered.

The constant influx of his emotions was overwhelming, increasing my anxiety. When my body started trembling, Storm casually leaned against me. She lowered her mental walls to allow me to take a few sips of her emotions and put my mind into a neutral, calm state. It was the only thing that worked to dull my senses—well, that and alcohol. Gratefully, I latched on to our connection to take the edge off my instability.

Desperate for her to soothe me through our bond, my heart dropped when my emotional state didn't change with each pull. It wasn't working. I tried not to panic as I quickly severed the link. My forehead dripped with sweat. I squirmed when I felt Ryker staring at me.

As if sensing my tension, he strode over and sat beside me. Now I was sandwiched between Ryker and Storm. He draped his arm behind me, lightly touching my neck. I froze when the unrelenting barrage of Burrows's emotions started to ebb away. I sighed, almost purring like a satisfied cat. Storm gasped, glancing at me before staring at Burrows.

Reason cleared her throat. "Detective, please get on with it."

He gritted his teeth. "I have a couple of questions for Lightning and Stormy Credence that I want answered."

Reason ruthlessly looked at him. "You will do well to remember that we've granted this meeting as a courtesy. You can ask all the questions you want, but they are not obligated to answer."

Burrows's body tightened. "Exactly in what capacity did Celina Rouse work for you?"

Storm looked at Reason, and she nodded.

Storm answered, "There's no magic to this, Detective. Our company caters to the rich and famous, and they pay us to provide beautiful women as arm candy at important events."

His eyes gleamed. "Go on."

I smiled. "What more do you want us to say, Detective? Our employees are beautiful women. Some are former models, including Celina. They pretty up an event. They are paid handsomely and get to connect with wealthy men. It's common among the rich. They want attractive and young, and we provide it."

"There's nothing scandalous or exciting about our company or our employees." Storm finished.

His eyes narrowed. "Except, according to my investigation, Celina's hobbies as a teenager included burglary, shoplifting, and grand theft."

I laughed. *What an idiot.* "Unlike you, we don't judge, Detective. Celina cleaned up her act years ago, before becoming employed by us."

"What do you know about her boyfriends?" He arched a brow. "According to a neighbor, he saw a man pounding on Celina's door before she was found dead."

Reason scoffed. "And that means what, Detective?"

"Maybe there was a little bit more going on that the Credence family knew about," he snapped. "The neighbors said she had a lot of men visiting at all hours of the night."

My mouth tightened. "Celina was young and beautiful. And what she did after-hours was her damn business."

Burrows's face flushed. "According to the reporter, Jeff Hunter, you were fully aware of what Celina did on her off hours. She was an escort, employed by you, to provide sexual favors to your clients."

Reason laughed. "All speculation, Detective."

Burrows's fists clenched. "Is this really how you bitches want to play it?"

Ryker's body tensed as he leaned forward with his hands on his knees, like he was about to leap forward and pounce on Burrows. "Detective Burrows, watch your damn mouth."

It was like a light bulb turned on, and all of Burrows's emotions pounded on me. He was writhing with pure hatred for everyone in the room. I nearly doubled over from pain. Ryker sharply looked at me and casually ran his cool fingers along my neck, like a caress. I almost sighed with relief when the pain ebbed away.

Burrows's hands shook as he snatched papers from his inner jacket pocket, erratically waving them. "Who do you people think you're fucking with? I received a copy of your client list from an anonymous source this morning. This list has more celebrities than the movie awards."

Storm responded coolly, "That means absolutely nothing."

"Nothing?" Burrows snarled. "Four of your clients are now lying in the morgue. All of them were found dead, their hearts ripped out. That's no coincidence."

We all blankly looked at him, which seemed to agitate him more.

Ryker and Knox stood up.

"Enough!" Ryker barked.

My head started pounding, feeling all of the sick, warped feelings circling in Burrows's head. He was fucking crazy.

Burrows stepped back, warily eyeballing Ryker and Knox before inspecting Storm and me.

He smiled spitefully. "Can you explain why you two were spotted in the reporter's neighborhood at the time of his death?"

Knox and Ryker exchanged a look.

Shit! Storm and I are in trouble.

"I'm sorry. You've lost me," Storm retorted.

"We found fingerprints all over his house," Burrows disclosed. "How much do you want to bet they're yours?"

"Impossible. We've never been there," I added quickly.

"Bloody fingerprints—his blood, your prints," he retorted confidently.

"Detective, where are you going with this?" Reason demanded.

He ignored her, looking over at us like a dog with a bone. "It's over. You killed a man."

Reason stiffly stood up. "If that were true, my clients would be in handcuffs, Detective. You have no evidence that my clients had anything to do with the murders. So if you even look at them the wrong way, lawsuit. If you try to contact any of their clients, lawsuit. If you even blink at them in a way that makes them a tad bit uncomfortable, lawsuit. Do you understand me,

Detective?" She nodded toward the door. "This interview is over."

My body tensed when I felt my mother and my aunt approaching. They were like a tornado—powerful and deadly, and touchdown to destruction was rapidly descending.

"I don't think you understand the gravity of the situation here. There were multiple homicides," Burrows proclaimed.

"Lawyer," Storm and I replied in unison.

Burrows turned bright red. "So are you lawyering up? Because—"

The office door crashed open, cutting off his tirade. Mom and Aunt Ava barged in with cool looks on their faces. Mom slammed the door shut, and they both nonchalantly looked at Burrows.

"Oh God! The witches have landed," Storm hissed under her breath.

"It seems like we're right on time, Ava," Mom surmised.

"Yes, it does, Lia," Aunt Ava responded.

Reason gestured toward Mom. "Lia Credence." She nodded over to my aunt. "Ava Credence." She sighed heavily. "They're Lightning's and Stormy's mothers and also their business partners."

Burrows looked at them with lustful eyes while extending his hand too eagerly. "Detective Burrows." He cleared his throat. "After I'm done with your daughters, I would love to question both of you privately."

Mom and Aunt Ava looked at his sweaty hand like it was a disgusting snake. Embarrassed, he pulled it back, wiping it on his jacket.

Aunt Ava smirked before taking out her cell phone. She flicked through her contacts list while coldly looking at him. She sighed as her phone dialed. "Hey, Todd! How are you?" She listened. "Yes. We just got back into town. It's too bad Salana missed the retreat." She paused. "You're a newlywed. I don't blame her." She laughed huskily. "Yes, she's hell on wheels . . .

exactly how you like it." She looked over at Burrows with distaste written all over her face. "Look, Todd, I have a shitty issue here." She paused dramatically. "A detective . . ." She arched a brow at my mom. "Uh, Lia, what is his name?"

"Burrows," Mom responded with a bored look.

"Uh, yes, there's a Detective Burrows." Aunt Ava looked him up and down. "He seems to have a bug that's crawled up his ass. And despite our attempts to be reasonable, he insists on stalking my family. It's creepy, to say the least." She smiled. "Thank you. And tell Salana we'll definitely do dinner this week." She hung up and turned her back on Burrows.

Rip stared at Soar with a smirk. "She's got the mayor on speed dial. This can't be good."

Detective Burrows's cell rang. He shifted uncomfortably before pulling it out. "Todd?" His face turned beet red. "Uh, I mean, Mayor Hannity. I—" He gritted his teeth. "You're kidding, right? They're suspects, and . . . Yes, sir. But your request is highly unusual. All I'm saying is you're asking me to walk away from an ongoing murder investigation." He paused. "Yes, sir. Murder. Several. One reporter. One woman who worked for them in a dubious capacity. And four clients. All dead in a span of one week, sir. Considering the nature of the crime scenes, I don't think it's a good idea to ask me not to pursue this further."

I stared at Burrows while trying to choke down the barrage of emotions he was emitting—anger, bitterness, deception. The man was a cesspool of crazy. His eyes burned with raw hatred as he scanned the room, deliberately stopping at me and staring. Suddenly, anxiety streamed from his pores.

"There are no issues," he snapped before Mayor Hannity hung up on him.

"Now, was that so hard?" I mumbled under my breath.

Burrows angrily looked at Aunt Ava and Mom. "I gotta hand it to you. This whole long con you've got going—it's impressive." His phone vibrated. He looked down at it, reading a text with a slow, icky smile spreading across his ruddy face. He looked slyly over at Ryker before glancing at Mom and Aunt Ava. "Did Mr. Alfero tell you he knew Celina Rouse . . . intimately?"

I felt Detective Burrows's desperation. Ryker's body tightened before he stepped forward. I wrapped my fingers around his arm, stopping him from kicking Burrows's ass. Burrows wanted to start some shit between us, and I'd be damned if I gave him the satisfaction.

Ryker considered me, relaxing his body. "I won't even dignify that bullshit accusation with a response, Detective."

"What in the hell is going on? You can't go in there!" Tabitha screamed from outside the office.

The door swung open. Burrows smiled at the younger man, who shoved an older man over the threshold before brazenly stepping in.

Soar slammed his hand against the man's chest, blocking him. "Hold on. Who the hell is this asshole?"

The man flashed his badge. "I'm Detective Peterson, Burrows's partner." He shoved the disheveled man forward again. "This is Leo Greco."

"I know my rights. You can't detain me without cause," Leo snapped in a light British accent.

I couldn't sense Leo's emotions. He was definitely an Other. But I read Peterson's emotions loud and clear—arrogance, resentment and bitterness.

"You are not under arrest . . . yet," Burrows replied.

"What is this shit?" Knox barked.

Burrows glared at Leo. "Do you recognize Mr. Alfero?"

Leo shrugged. "Like I told you, I don't know him." His eyes defiantly shifted from Ryker to Jackal and then back to Burrows. "Why the hell am I here? I don't know anything about these people. You dragged me out of my hotel room for fucking nothing. I'm on vacation, man."

Ryker's eyes narrowed, as if realizing the larger implications of Leo's presence.

"Drop the act, Leo. An informant sent us a picture of you

casing the Credence home one week ago," Burrows barked before nodding at Peterson, who pulled a photo out of his jacket and showed it to Leo. "That is you, isn't it?"

Leo slapped the photo. It dropped to the floor. "Whenever I come to New York, I always like to take the time to admire the city's neighborhoods. Is that a crime?"

Reason calmly picked up the photo, examined it, and handed it over to Aunt Ava and Mom.

Peterson nodded, but it was clear he didn't believe the excuse.

Burrows scowled. "You're a liar. You burglarized the Credence safe."

"Excellent. We would love to know why he stole our business documents and exactly where they are," Storm commented.

Peterson smugly watched Ryker. "You know Leo."

Burrows had an annoyed expression on his face while surveying Ryker. "I will give you this; you've got some gigantic balls. You're playing the Credence family while pretending to be their ally."

Ryker had a blank expression. "If you have something to say, spit it out."

Burrows's eyes narrowed. "We've obtained a warrant for your financials, and we will find evidence of the money you paid Mr. Greco to disable the security system at the Credence home."

"Bullshit!" Ryker sneered.

My eyes snapped over to Ryker.

Reason pointed to the door. "Detective Burrows, get the hell out. I will not allow this circus to continue."

Jackal, Rip, and Soar moved closer to the detectives, menacingly scowling at them.

Burrows gaped at Ryker. "We'll see about that." He looked at Storm and me with a crazed expression in his eyes. "I'll be seeing you . . . soon. Come on, Peterson."

He stomped over to the door before flinging it open. Peterson started to drag Leo toward the door.

Ryker looked at Reason.

She cleared her throat. "Since Mr. Greco is not under arrest, he stays."

Burrows nodded toward the hallway. "Leo, can I talk to you for a minute? In private."

He looked at Ryker and then his enforcers. "Nope."

Burrows glared at Leo. "Don't leave New York." He gave Leo one more glare before he and Peterson stomped out.

We all stared at Leo while he shuffled nervously as Jackal, Rip, and Soar surrounded him.

"Talk, hyena," Ryker barked. "Who hired you to steal the Credence client list?"

I glanced at Ryker, his distaste for Leo clearly written on his face. Burrows was right; they did know each other. I looked over at Mom and Aunt Ava. My eyes widened. They seemed to know Leo, too.

Leo was a strange-looking man . . . hyena thing. He looked a little like a weasel. He was not quite my height, thin but leanly muscled. His face was plain, easily overlooked. But those beady predator eyes took in everything and everyone in the room.

"I wasn't hired to steal the client list. My contact told me I was being paid to test their security for vulnerabilities. I was to break in, disable the alarm, and walk out undetected. And for my trouble, I got fifty grand in advance," Leo confessed.

"Who hired you?" Aunt Ava demanded.

He shrugged. "I don't know and don't care. Everything goes through a third party. It's safer that way," Leo defended while anxiously looking toward the door.

"Mmm, yeah, until you get set up. The real thief needed you to disable the alarms," Soar observed.

"Yeah, apparently," Leo stated flatly.

Something about his shifty demeanor set my teeth on edge. "What did you see at our house?" I questioned.

His beady eyes probed me with interest.

I scoffed. "Oh, so not going to happen, hyena."

"Nothing at first. I mean, it all went too easy. I got halfway back to the car when it hit me. I had already disabled the alarms, right? And it was . . . sitting there," Leo divulged.

"You went back for the rest of the money in the safe?" Ryker interrogated.

"Well, there's an awful lot of temptation, all that money and jewelry. When I got back into the house, there was a woman walking toward the safe. So I got the bloody hell out of there," Leo stated.

Aunt Ava curiously looked at him. "This woman, what did she look like?"

"I barely got a glimpse," Leo responded. "All I can say for sure is she was a wolf-shifter. I smelled the doggy stench a mile away."

Ryker stared at him before saying, "Soar, take Leo outside and have a conversation with him about not leaving town until we tell him to. I want him to know exactly what will happen to him if he makes me come searching for him."

Soar shoved Leo out the door.

Knox scrutinized Storm. "Why didn't you tell me that you and Light went to the reporter's house?"

"There was nothing to say. Ryker told us to take care of the situation, and we did. We went over there, but his house had already been broken into, and he was dead. We picked up the copies of our client list and documents and got the hell out of there," Storm reported with an annoyed look on her face.

Ryker angrily looked at me. "Burrows said your fingerprints were all over his house. Why is that?"

Barely holding in my temper, I crossed my arms. "If you're insinuating that we killed him, then you're on some shit, Wolfie. Burrows lied. We touched nothing. But why someone wants to implicate us for killing him . . . that's something my family will find out." I paused. "Your presence here is no longer needed. The Credence family takes care of their own."

"He's not going anywhere. We invited him here," Mom

snapped. "This is serious. You two have singlehandedly destroyed the family business in a matter of days."

I rolled my eyes. "Mom, please use your inside voice."

"This is my damn inside voice. Ryker told us what happened with Luke." She scrutinized Storm. "You are fucking lucky that idiot didn't kill you."

"What in the hell were you thinking, Storm? You went to see him by yourself?" Aunt Ava snapped.

"Mom, I had it handled," Storm hissed.

"Handled? You were damn lucky Knox found you before Luke Brasson killed you."

"Why are you . . . ?" I trailed off when I realized. "Wait, how did you know his last name?"

Mom shrugged. "There isn't a damn thing we don't know. Luke is the only descendant of Morpheus Brasson. The Brassons are the bloodline of warlocks who are prominent members of the Shadows."

Storm's mouth dropped open. "Hold on a minute. Exactly what do you know about the Shadows?"

"What are the Shadows?" I replied.

Mom impatiently tapped her stiletto. "We don't have time for a history lesson, Light."

"Make time," Storm snapped.

"You two are damn pains in the ass," Mom scolded before sighing heavily. "The Shadows are ancient fae groupies. Essentially, they are a group of warlocks who worshipped the ground our ancestors walked on." She shook her head in dismay. "They did some really crazy things to show their devotion to the fae. They even offered their wives to them in hopes that the fae would breed with them, but thank goodness, the fae refused. Shit went to hell when the fae disappeared. That's when the Shadows started stalking our family, obsessed with breeding with us to create a new race of fae." Mom finished sharply.

"And at what point were you going to let us know about them?" Storm screamed angrily. "Light and I had the right to know about the Shadows. Luke told me the Credence curse was a bunch of bullshit. There was never a curse. Dammit, come on, guys. For centuries, the Shadows have been stalking us, killing every man we loved, and you blamed it on a fucking curse."

"We did what we had to . . . to protect you," Aunt Ava confided.

I stood up, jamming my fists on my hips. "No. You did what you did to protect some bullshit Credence secret," I snapped.

Storm huffed with frustration. "I was almost killed by Luke."

My eyes narrowed. I didn't like the sound of this. "What happened with Luke?"

"Somehow, he got my cell number and called me while I was at Knox's house. I was about to hang up when he started raving like a lunatic." Storm ran her hands through her hair. "He ranted about why the Credence women insisted on whoring themselves to humans."

Aunt Ava calmly looked at her. "The Shadows are fanatics."

"They sound more like nuts," I stated.

"They are psychos. Thinking about the crazed look in Luke's eyes makes my blood boil. He went on some crazy tirade, actually talking to himself, insisting the men of the Shadows were born to love only us." She looked over at Knox. "He actually killed the reporter . . . for me. And I fucking panicked, thinking about the likelihood of him killing Knox."

"The Shadows believe when the fae left, the Credence family was their gift to the Shadows." Mom revealed.

Aunt Ava pursed her lips. "All bullshit, of course."

"They want to procreate with the Credence bloodline?" Knox snarled.

My jaw tightened. "I would rather render myself childless than procreate with those psychos."

"Fortunately, every time they tried to infiltrate our family, we stopped them," Mom disclosed.

I closed my eyes, pushing down the building rage for the way the Shadows had killed without remorse. Throughout the centuries, those killings had caused Credence women to suffer needlessly, with some of them going damn near insane from the burden of the Credence Curse. It was cruel and inhumane.

"Do you think your clients were killed by the Shadows?" Ryker questioned.

"That's what we intend on finding out," Mom stated. "The only thing puzzling me is the fact that the Shadows have never been this brazen. Now I'm rethinking everything. Luke outed himself to Storm, so obviously, their strategy has changed."

Ryker looked at Mom and Aunt Ava. "Unfortunately, we are both caught between a rock and a hard place. The Other Council was already in an uproar about the stolen client list. Now, with your clients dead, the Council has voted to shut down Credence O., pending the completion of a formal investigation." His eyes hardened. "And this is nonnegotiable."

I absolutely hated the Other Council. They were the governing body of the Others who helped enforce the most important rule—Others did not reveal their existence to humans. Too many members of the Council had an ax to grind with my family for one irrational reason or another.

"You're the leader of the Other Council. You can explain to them that this shit is bigger than the Credence family. Our missing client list affects everyone, regardless of who they blame for the list being stolen in the first place," I stated.

Ryker laughed bitterly. "What do you want me to tell the council? That a group of lunatics is stalking your family? I tell them that shit, and they will push for a permanent shutdown in addition to exiling your family. Come on. Others are already paranoid enough. This will only give them an excuse to blame you for outing Others."

Mom sighed tiredly. "Under other circumstances, we would fight this suspension, but there is no such thing as coincidences. Our client list being stolen, Celina's, the reporter's, and our clients' deaths, combined with Luke trying to kill Storm—it's all hitting too close to home."

Aunt Ava's eyes turned deadly. "Trust me; we'll get to the bottom of this."

"Whether it's the Shadows or someone else, it's not only a Credence problem anymore. Whoever is doing this is fucking up my plan for an Others peace treaty." Ryker's eyes impaled me. "You might not like me, but I'm trying to help figure this crap out without starting an Others war. Believe me; I'm the lesser of the evils out there."

"Seeing is believing, given the bad blood between our families, alpha," I bellowed.

Mom sharply appraised me. "Light! Ryker is not our enemy. He called us. He didn't have to. He could have been an asshole, like the rest of the council."

"Besides, the bad blood between our families was buried with Tiber and Solista," Aunt Ava snapped.

I snorted.

Tiber Alfero, Ryker's great-grandfather, had gone down in history as the most ruthless wolf-shifter who ever lived. He was also known as a notorious womanizer, who had strung Solista Credence, my great-grandmother, around for years.

Storm's eyes narrowed. "Is it?"

"What the hell is that supposed to mean, Storm?" Knox demanded.

"There's a little bit more to the story between Tiber and Solista," Storm offered, her eyes darting to me.

"And how would you know that?" Mom commented suspiciously.

"Uh . . . Light, don't freak out, okay?" Storm smiled nervously.

I didn't like the sound of this. "Freak out about what?"

"Well . . ." Storm paused, nervously licking her lips. "Don't ask me how . . . but Tiber pulled me into some creepy realm between the human realm and the Others realm."

I blinked. "And how the hell did he do that?"

She shrugged. "He said the ancient fae granted him the gift of bringing me there."

Ryker impatiently inspected her. "For what?"

My jaw tightened. "Exactly. For what? His great-grandfather turned his back on Great-Grandmother Solista when she needed him."

Ryker flinched, widening his stance. "He paid for his blunder. Get past it."

I crossed my arms, not giving an inch. "What did he want? Forgiveness for his mistakes?"

Storm scratched her head. "Well . . . I don't really know. He said you and I are the bond that ties the Alfero pack together."

I arched a brow. "There's no bond with that pack."

"He seemed to think so. He was worried about the survival of his bloodline—and warned that the Shadows were planning to cleanse the world of what they deemed a blight of nature."

"Oh God, don't tell me. They want to eliminate all Others," I muttered.

"Yep."

My mouth dropped open. *Oh damn, this isn't good.*

Storm continued. "He said our bond is the only thing preventing this destruction from happening."

Ryker deliberately said nothing, letting the cooling sound of silence speak volumes.

"So it's true. You and Light are the only Credence women to be gifted with fae powers." Mom proudly looked at Aunt Ava.

"Uh, I don't want fae powers. I don't even want the power I already have." It would be another burden to carry, and I'd had enough with the empath affliction looming over me like the Grim Reaper. I dropped my head in my hands. *Damn, please don't let me freak.*

The buzzing of Mom's cell interrupted my slow slide into depression.

Mom glanced down at her phone. "What the hell?" she

barked into the phone. "Who is this?" She paused. "Raphael?" Her voice hitched.

Aunt Ava's body stiffened.

Mom's face turned red. She was seriously distressed. I'd never seen my unflappable mom like this.

"Who's Raphael?" I asked Aunt Ava.

She ignored me, visibly shaken.

Mom tightly smiled at us. "Excuse me for a minute," she mumbled before gliding out of the office.

Ryker nodded over to Rip.

Rip nodded back. "On it." He strode out of the office after her.

I glanced at Storm. "What the hell was that about?"

Storm shrugged. "Damn if I know. But it sure didn't look good."

❧ 5 ☙

LIGHTNING

Fifteen nail-biting minutes later, Mom burst into the office as if nothing had happened. I knew better. Something had left her on edge.

I suspiciously looked over at her. "Is everything all right?"

She smiled tightly. "Nothing we can't deal with."

Soar and Rip appeared in the doorway.

"The hyena is all squared away," Soar assured Ryker.

"Good," Ryker responded. "Rip, we'll talk later."

Rip's eyes swept over to Mom and then back at him. "You bet we will."

Jackal's phone rang. He moved to the farthest corner of the room. "Are you sure?" He paused. "Who?" He listened while running a hand over his head. "You've got to be fucking kidding me. Get back to me when you get more info." He hung up his phone, grimly watching us. "That was my connection. He wanted me to know that they picked up some strange chatter on the Others network. There's a two-hundred-thousand-dollar contract on the Credence family," he stated calmly.

"The shit keeps on getting better and better," Storm declared.

Mom's back straightened. "What kind of contract?"

"Don't know. He's still working on the intel."

Ryker stared at them. "Ava, Lia, be fucking straight with me. What the hell is this really about?"

Mom exhaled noisily. "You know what this is about—the Shadows."

Knox crossed his arms, widening his stance. "Then we protect them. I have a tour I'm contractually obligated to go on, so I'm taking Storm with me."

Storm sighed heavily. "No asking, just telling. We are going to have to work on your relationship skills, rock star." She paused. "I'll go with you. It's not like I have a job to go to until this whole mess is cleaned up." She worriedly peered over at me. "But Light's coming with me."

My eyes widened. "Fuck no! I'm not going to be some third wheel."

I watched Knox grab Storm's hand, tenderly kissing it. Storm reached up and touched his face. *Fuck, these two are in love and need time to cement their relationship.* And there was no way I was going to stay with my mom and Aunt Ava. I would end up killing the annoying witches.

"I'll stay with Reason," I said.

Storm sputtered, "What?"

Aunt Ava looked at me like I'd lost my damn mind. "No. Reason can't protect you. Besides, we don't want to put her in danger. Her father will kill us." She looked at Ryker. "You will protect her until we figure this shit out."

"Like I have a choice," Ryker responded while glaring at me.

Arguing with them was futile. They were right; Reason's father was overly protective of her, and he would lose his shit if she got hurt over our issues.

Reason pursed her lips. "Hey, people, I'm standing right here. I can bring in my father's enforcers."

"Oh, hell no! No vampires. We can't trust the bloodsuckers," Soar retorted.

"You're saying I can't be trusted?" Reason countered.

"Exactly."

I threw up my hands, exasperated. "Stop, you two. You're giving me a damn headache. I'll stay with Wolfie." I grimaced at Ryker. "But understand, I'm not putting up with any of your shit."

He coldly stared at me. "You want my protection, you live with my rules. And that shit is not negotiable."

I glared at him. "We'll see about that."

Mom and Aunt Ava eyed each other.

"Well, this should be interesting," Aunt Ava concluded wryly.

Mom eyeballed Ryker. "Guys, we need a minute with our daughters."

"Don't take long. I have business to take care of," Ryker barked before they all filed out of the office.

"So was that who I think it was?" Aunt Ava asked Mom with an anxious expression.

"Yes, Light's father," Mom stated matter-of-factly.

My body stiffened. "What the hell are you talking about?" Of anything Mom could have said, I hadn't expected that. "You told me he was dead."

Mom completely ignored me and looked directly at Aunt Ava. "They know."

Aunt Ava gasped. "Holy shit!"

"Why are you ignoring me?" I huffed angrily. "And who's *they*?" I demanded.

Ava sighed tiredly. "Lia, tell Light the truth. We can't shield her from it anymore."

Mom reached for me, and I pulled away. "Your father is not dead. We told you that to protect you from them."

"Who the hell is *them*?"

She sighed tiredly. "The Shadows." She paused. "I—"

I interrupted her. "Okay, what else did you lie about?" I was damn near hysterical. My heart was racing as my fingers tingled strangely.

Mom gritted her teeth. "Stop it! First, I've never lied to you."

"You told me he was dead. Now you're saying he's alive. Which is it?"

Storm plopped down onto the sofa. "Shit! I can't cope with all this drama."

Mom paced back and forth. "It's complicated."

I clenched and unclenched my fists. "Then uncomplicate it, Mother."

"Raphael, your father, is the only son of the leader of the Shadows." She shrugged. "I fell in love with him."

"Before you start squawking, she didn't know Raphael was his son," Aunt Ava argued.

Mom interrupted her. "We loved each other. When he revealed the truth, I was already pregnant with you. The only way he could make sure you wouldn't fall into the hands of his father and the Shadows was to disappear. He did it to protect you and me."

I couldn't hide my shock and confusion. "I don't understand. Why do they want me?"

"You're special. You're the only empath alive"—she paused—"with the ability to control all Others."

"Control? Wait. What?" I swallowed. "Hold on. How can I be the only damn empath?" That was like saying I was a unicorn.

"There are those who have some empath abilities, like Ava, Storm, and me. But our powers are limited. To mix our bloodline with the Shadows' dark bloodline is like a Molotov cocktail."

"What do you mean dark?" I asked quickly.

"Dark magic. They have bred with evil underworld beings. Some real dark, evil shit. That's what makes their magic so powerful."

"And that's why if you are in the wrong hands—the Shadows' hands—it can do irreparable damage."

My eyes widened. "Fuck! They're coming after me. How did they find out who I am?"

Mom's mouth tightened. "Because your father was careless. Somehow, they found out about him and you and that he was alive and back in New York, watching you." She sighed. "Fucking overprotective ass." She rubbed her head. "Raphael knew they'd come for you. That's why he called to warn us."

I paced back and forth with my mind racing. I felt Mom's, Aunt Ava's, and Storm's heated stares. I didn't give a shit. I was trying to work out my own issues . . . for once.

"Light, is everything okay with you?" Storm asked.

"I'm fine."

"Say something, sweetie," Aunt Ava demanded.

I strode faster. "No, I don't have anything to say." I skidded to a stop. "You know what? I do have something to say. All these years, and you never once thought about telling me the truth?" I didn't bother to hide the hurt and the tears that threatened to fall. "I get it. I understand why you and my father—I mean, Raphael did what you did. But you want to know what hurts me more? The fact that you lied to me." My mouth twisted with disdain. "All that bullshit about no secrets in the family, and every damn day, you lied to me because you didn't think I could handle the truth." I was truly disgusted with Mom and Aunt Ava.

Nothing was taboo in my family. We were progressively open about sex. We had to be with the nature of our business. The things I was able to discuss with my mom and my aunt at a young age would make humans cringe. There wasn't anything that wasn't up for discussion—or so I'd thought.

Mom gave me an incredulous stare. "This is not all about you. There's the whole family's safety to consider. Sweetie, I know you could have handled the truth, but you'll soon discover the Credence women sometimes have to do things we're not too proud of . . . and make sacrifices for the betterment of all, not one."

I processed her words. I loved my family and would do anything in my power to protect them, even at the expense of my own happiness and safety. That was, after all, how the Credence family had survived all these years—by making sacrifices. There were times we'd fight bitterly, but we always stood together in the end. We were the Credences. And I would be damned if I let the Shadows or Raphael tear my family apart.

Mom, Aunt Ava, and Storm opened their arms. I stepped forward for the group hug. I basked in the strength of their love, knowing the times ahead were going to be rough for all of us.

I sighed, stepping back. "So what now?"

Mom pushed the hair back from my face. "We stick to the plan. Storm will go with Knox. Ava and I will call in a few favors to get some extra protection for us. And since Ryker has graciously offered to protect you, you will go with him."

I arched a brow. "Graciously? The man hates me." I didn't know how in the hell I was going to last with Ryker as my jail warden. Shit, I didn't know whether to fuck him or kick his ass. I huffed out with displeasure. *And what is the deal with my human emotional angst subsiding when he's around me? Is it the fae thing kicking in or something else altogether?*

Aunt Ava beamed. "He doesn't hate you."

I threw my hands in the air. "What is it with you two and Ryker? He's not some cute puppy you can play with. I've seen behind his cool demeanor. He's damn near feral."

Mom's eyes narrowed. "I see."

I blinked. "You . . . see? What exactly do you see?"

Mom shrewdly considered. "That you're afraid of him."

I sputtered, "I'm not afraid of him. I'm stating a fact. His wolf, his beast, is chained inside his body like some sort of dangerous animal."

Storm stared at me, confused. "You saw that?"

I glared at her like she'd lost her damn mind. "What the hell is wrong with you? Of course I didn't see it." I bit my bottom lip. "I sensed it," I blurted out before I could stop myself.

Storm shook her head. "Now you can 'sense'"—she did air quotes—"Others' emotions?"

I gave up. I had to tell them the truth. "Not Others'. His."

They stared with open mouths.

"Briefly. Oh, okay, once at his charity gala."

They arched their brows.

"And again today, but it was brief. Strange and unrepeatable."

"Uh-huh," Mom quipped.

Aunt Ava gawked at Mom. "This is . . ."

"Surprising." Mom finished.

I hated when they did the dynamic-duo shit, finishing each other's sentences and thoughts.

I loudly snapped my fingers. "None of that."

"What?" they retorted in unison.

I rolled my eyes. "Like I said, Ryker is fucking feral."

Aunt Ava sternly gazed at me. "Hey, we raised you better than that. No judging different." She gestured to each of us. "We're all different. He's different, but he's not feral. He's the descendant of Loki, the Norse god. And he's fighting not to be as destructive and ruthless as his ancestors. It's not easy."

Mom clucked her tongue. "We all have demons we're fighting." She blankly studied me. "He needs to find his balance to end his pain."

"I'm sorry. When did we start giving a shit about the Alferos?" I asked.

Mom crossed her arms. "I don't understand why you have this uncanny ability to run when you have the remote chance of forming an emotional connection with any man."

"I've learned from the best," I replied while giving them both a pointed stare.

"Ryker is different."

I rolled my eyes. "Different? He's an arrogant ass with a condescending air." I mockingly tapped my chin. "Let me think . . . That sounds like a typical alpha wolf-shifter. There's nothing special about him; believe me."

Mom smirked. "He's unique. You have to give him a chance."

I was so done with this conversation. "I have no intention of giving him a chance."

"Has it ever occurred to you that maybe Ryker is worth pursuing as mating material?" Aunt Ava asked.

"Nope. I don't do permanent. Shit, no one in this family, besides Storm, is even capable of doing long-term relationships. I've seen the look in his eyes. All he wants is another sexual conquest."

Mom and Aunt Ava smirked at each other.

Mom shooed me with her hand. "He doesn't know what he needs right now. He's thinking with his cock, but he'll soon realize what he needs is a little more complicated."

My eyes narrowed. "What are you two up to?"

Mom winked at me. "Nothing, sweetie."

"Right." I paused. "You know what? It doesn't matter," I proclaimed.

Aunt Ava picked up her cell and started to text. "Exactly."

I looked at Storm. She did the crazy sign, making a circling motion with her index finger at the side of her head.

Mom looked at her watch. "It's time to go. You two, please try to be on your best behavior. We'll handle the investigation."

"And we'll sit around twiddling our thumbs?" Storm snapped.

"Hell no! This has to do with us, too," I insisted.

Mom's mouth tightened. "I don't give a flying fuck. Don't mess with me, Light. We'll handle this. You stay out of this." She sternly looked at Storm. "You, too." Something in her expression told us she wasn't hopeful, but she didn't have time to dwell.

Aunt Ava hugged us both. "Thank God they're going to be separated. It'll be less trouble for them to get into while the Shadows stalk us."

I incredulously looked at them. "Wait. You're using us as bait?"

Aunt Ava playfully pulled my hair. "We're all bait, Light."

Storm rolled her eyes. "You know what happens to bait? It eventually gets eaten."

Mom's and Aunt Ava's faces tightened.

"That's what we're counting on," Mom remarked.

"Give your enemies enough rope, and they'll hang themselves. And when they do, we'll finish them off for good." Aunt Ava finished.

Mom headed straight for me and grabbed my face. She kissed my cheek. "Be safe, okay?" she whispered. "Please don't do anything to get yourself in trouble, okay?"

I rubbed my head. If they thought I was going to sit around and wait for the Shadows to get me, they had another thing coming. "I'm not making any promises. Love you."

We hugged each other again before Mom and Aunt Ava exited.

Storm grabbed me and hugged me hard. I hugged her back, kissing her on the cheek. We both were emotional.

This wasn't how we'd wanted this to go. We had grown up together, gone to college together, worked together, and traveled all over the world together. And at twenty-four years of existence, we had more money than either of us could spend. But money couldn't buy love or happiness.

It was time, time for us to forge our own way.

She had Knox now, and I wanted her to be happy. She fucking deserved it. And there was no doubt in my mind that Knox would make sure she would never want for anything . . . love, affection, protection, and happiness. He was truly a fucking good guy.

"I love you," Storm whispered.

"I love you, too."

Storm pulled back with a hint of worry in her eyes. I reassuringly squeezed her arm. She was used to fixing my problems, and up until now, I had been quite happy to allow her to. But things had changed. The situation had changed. I was changing. I wasn't sure whether it was for better or worse.

"We'll talk every night. I'll be waiting to hear all the scandalous things you've done to the alpha," Storm teased.

I gave her a devilish grin. "Oh, you can count on that shit. Project Make Wolfie's Life a Living Hell starts as soon as I walk out of this damn office."

"Give him hell." She pinched my cheek. She looked over her shoulder at Knox leaning against the wall, talking to Ryker. "I gotta go."

She gave me a small smile. I returned it.

I stood there for a minute, never feeling as alone as I felt right then. I watched Storm exit the office and into the arms of Knox. I smiled. They were so in love. I was content to bask in the warmth of their new love, when the alpha from hell turned around and scowled at me.

"Are you coming or what?" he snapped.

I sighed heavily before marching toward him. "Would it kill you to say something polite for once?"

He growled.

I reached up and tapped his cheek—hard. "Good thing I'll be staying with you for a long time. It will give me plenty of time to teach you some manners . . . Lightning style." I grinned. "Now come along, Wolfie. Time's a-wastin'."

When I heard his teeth grinding, I sauntered away with an extra pep in my step.

Yep, let the games begin.

$$\clubsuit \quad 6 \quad \clubsuit$$

LIGHTNING

It was wishful thinking that the Neanderthal I now called Ryker would say at least one word to me on the ride over to Alfero headquarters. It would have made the ride less boring. But, no, Ryker spent the whole ride alternating between texting and talking on his phone. *Shit! The man never stops working.* There were nonstop calls about his pack, the Other Council, and his company. No wonder he was so uptight.

I sighed with relief when we pulled up to his headquarters. The driver opened the door, and Ryker whisked me into the building.

Bones, one of his enforcers, was standing in the lobby, flirting with the receptionist. He turned around, and his lips curled into an easy smile as he maintained eye contact. "Well, if it isn't Lightning Credence."

I boldly checked out his athletic build and chocolate-brown hair. *Oh, yippee, a nice new toy to play with.* "Well, if it isn't the cowboy I call Bones," I mimicked with a Southern drawl.

Ryker's unflinchingly piercing gaze met Bones's with a frown. "Is everything ready upstairs?"

Bones's smile disappeared, looking from Ryker to me with interest. "Yes . . ." He cleared his throat. "But there's a problem."

Ryker pushed me toward the waiting elevator. "What problem?" he snapped as all three of us entered the elevator. The door closed, and it instantly began moving.

Bones uncomfortably looked at me and then back at him. "Sophie showed up. And she's in your office, refusing to leave."

Ryker scowled as the elevator opened. "I don't need this shit right now."

I tried not to flinch when he put his hand on the small of my back, guiding me into the sleek office space. His headquarters occupied one floor of a mammoth office building in the Garment District. With its thirty-ninth–floor views of Times Square and West Side Manhattan, his office was bigger than most New York apartments and lavishly tasteful. The sitting area had leather couches and an elaborate coffee table where art books were piled. A large flat-screen TV on one wall was tuned silently to the news channel.

A distressed woman came bustling toward Ryker. "I apologize, Mr. Alfero. She just showed up. God, that woman is so infuriating," the woman commented.

I heard the elevator ding, and the doors opened, revealing the dynamic trio of Jackal, Rip, and Soar, who barreled toward us like a freight train.

"What's going on?" Rip asked.

"Sophie. And she's in Ryker's office," the woman whispered.

I curiously looked at them. *Why are they so worked up about Sophie?*

"I'll take care of this." Ryker nodded toward me. "Soar, take her to the lounge and then prepare the conference room. I want to see the footage. I'll be right back."

He started to prowl toward his office, with Rip, Jackal, and Bones following close behind him.

"Oh no, you don't!" I grabbed his arm, prettily smiling at him. "You promised to protect me. So where you go, I go. That's the deal, alpha, and that's not negotiable," I mocked before pushing past them. "Besides, I want to meet Sophie. She sounds like lots of fun."

"You're with me, darling." Ryker wrapped his arms around my waist, pulling me back against his body. His lips grazed the shell of my ear as he whispered, "I can't have you walking in on an unpredictable she-wolf."

The surprising contact made my nipples harden and my breathing increase as dampness soaked my underwear.

"What a gentleman," I huskily pointed out.

Abruptly, he released his grip, and a big-as-saucer hand rested comfortably on my hip, guiding me forward as he pushed open the door with me pinned to his side. I scanned the office, taking in the massive mahogany pieces dominating two walls and a large desk holding down one end of the room. My perusal skidded to a stop, and my eyes widened at the sight of a butt-naked Sophie kneeling in a submissive position.

"Happy birthday . . . sir!" Sophie addressed with her eyes still cast downward.

"Shit!" Ryker bit out.

"Oh my!" I bit my bottom lip to prevent myself from bursting out in a fit of giggles. "What do we have here?" I looked at him with fake shock. "Is she here to blow out your candle?"

Sophie's head jerked up. She glowered at me with frosty eyes. "Who is she?"

Rip laughed loudly. "Why can't shit like this ever happen to me?"

Jackal pushed farther into the office with an aloof stare. "It does but in the confines of the strip club you visit every month."

Ryker growled, "What the fuck is going on, Sophie?"

I winked at him. "I'm not judging. But next time, give a girl some warning before you bring out the sex freaks." I tapped my lip. "Now that I think of it, is there anything else you want to warn me about before I move into your penthouse?" I pointedly stared at Sophie. "Because I plan on being there for a long time."

Sophie stood up, not even bothering to pull on her clothes. I rolled my eyes. Modest she was not.

Sophie tossed her shiny waist-length blond hair over her shoulder, sneering at me. I stared at her tall, reed-thin body with peaches-and-cream skin and pouty mouth. Now I knew what type of women the alpha was into. She pushed out her clearly fake breasts that were hanging on a body so skinny I wished I had a cracker to give the poor starved soul.

"She's staying with you?" Sophie hotly jabbed a finger over at me. "Not once have you invited me to your place."

I wagged my finger at her like a schoolteacher. "And that should be a hint and a half for your ass. If a man doesn't invite you over to his place, you're definitely *not* a keeper."

"Why, you little bitch." Sophie lunged at me.

In a flash, Ryker stepped in front of me, blocking my view, and Rip and Jackal protectively flanked my sides. I shot them an annoyed stare. She-wolf or not, I could take on Sophie without even breaking a damn sweat.

"I don't have time for this shit. Sophie, put on your clothes and get out," Ryker barked impatiently.

I determinedly pushed past Ryker and strolled by her before sinking into Ryker's buttery leather office chair with a sigh of exaggerated contentment. "Don't mind me." I waved a hand. "I'll be quiet. I love watching a good freak show."

Sophie's eyes narrowed bitterly before she marched over to Ryker, grabbing his arm. I yawned at her clear attempt at possession, but deep down inside, something I never experienced before stirred within me—jealousy. I curled my fingers against my thighs to prevent myself from jumping up and slapping her hands off him.

Ryker frowned while peeling Sophie's hand off him. "Sophie, what the hell are you playing at?"

Sophie's mouth tightened. "Ryker, who is this?"

He growled, "Sophie, you're testing my damn patience."

I crossed my legs while flirtatiously twirling a strand of hair.

"She wants to know if you and I are"—I looked up and smiled sexily—"fucking," I whispered loudly.

Rip laughed raucously. "God, this is funny."

Sophie sized me up. "Exactly," she hissed before jamming her hands on her hips while impatiently tapping her foot.

Ryker crossed his beefy arms. "That's none of your damn business." He nodded to her scattered clothes. "Now put on your damn clothes and get the hell out. You're embarrassing yourself."

Sophie huffed angrily.

"And the answer to your question is"—I saucily winked at Ryker—"not yet, but I'm working on it."

He smirked, and then he caught himself and frowned.

I continued. "And you should be damn worried when I do."

Sophie put her clothes on with angry, jerky movements.

"Because what's between my legs is so good that, if I threw it up in the air, it would make sunshine."

Jackal's mouth dropped open. "I'm going to need a cold shower."

"Shit. My cock just got rock hard," Rip mumbled.

Ryker scowled at them. "Don't encourage her."

Sophie snarled. "This is ridiculous."

I smiled like I'd won the lottery. "Ridiculously good. Now run along. Your services are not required"—I looked at Ryker with cold eyes—"anymore."

Sophie gasped.

Ryker crossed his arms. "Sophie, leave."

Her overinflated lips pouted before she pulled on her coat. "I'm not leaving. She is."

I smiled, enjoying the drama much more than I really should have. "Sweetie, your cheap shoes are over there." I pointed over to the door. "Put them on and skedaddle." I leaned forward, giving her the stare. "You're making the big, bad alpha and his sidekicks really uncomfortable."

She grabbed her shoes before marching over to me. "You can't have him," she snapped while pointing in my face.

Oh, hell no! There were a multitude of ways I could handle this, but the one I was leaning toward was breaking her skinny finger for being so unbelievably rude. I decided to take the high road, though—which, frankly, was highly unusual for me. Besides, Sophie was rearing for a fight that she had absolutely no chance of winning.

"Okay, first, the finger, get it out of my damn face. Second, you'd better be happy I don't really want Ryker"—I glared—"because I don't lose men. I collect them." I subtly tilted my head. "Now move your scrawny butt out of my face before I go straight New York on your ass."

Ryker strode over and guided Sophie toward the door. "Sophie, I don't play games."

She sputtered while maliciously looking at me, "You're kicking me out for this chubby bitch?"

I jumped up. "Okay, that's it. I tried to be nice, but the name-calling is the last straw."

Jackal and Rip dragged a cursing Sophie out of the office before quietly closing the door.

I venomously stared at him while throwing paper clips in the air. "Happy birthday, Wolfie!"

7

RYKER

PISSED OFF, I entered the soundproofed conference room, with Jackal and Rip trailing behind me. I stepped over the threshold and nodded at Jackal, who shut the door. Jackal, the second-highest-ranking member of my team, and Rip, the third, sat down, Jackal to my left and Rip to my right. The remaining member of the team, Soar, sat engrossed in pulling up data on his tablet.

"I've never witnessed anything as hot but frightening as what I just saw. And I'm not talking about Sophie," Jackal reported.

"God, every time Light opens her mouth, I don't know whether to run or beg her to make me her sexual submissive." Rip chuckled.

"What the fuck? Can you guys focus?" I snarled.

I was already regretting making the promise to protect Light. She was too much of a distraction.

Soar glanced up from his tablet. "What happened?"

"An epic clash of the Titans. Sophie, zero. Light, ten," Rip related.

Soar scowled. "Figures. Underneath that pretty face is a mean, vicious siren." He shook his head with a look of amazement. "Did you see what she did with that damn letter opener?

Fuck . . . inches away from taking out my eye." He smirked. "I would bring that woman to a knife fight any damn day."

I frowned. Soar was distrustful of everyone until he warmed up to them, and that could take months. Now he was an official member of the I Love Lightning fan club and way ahead of schedule.

Pressing my hands on the table, I allowed my power to roll off my body. "Enough! We have too much shit going on to be talking about Light and her damn antics." I took a cleansing breath before sitting down.

Rip laughed. "Man, you're just mad 'cause she won't kneel at your feet like every other woman."

Jackal grinned at me. "Let me give you some advice. This one is a wild stallion. Don't try to mind fuck her, 'cause it ain't going to work. A firm but gentle hand is needed to corral her into your bed."

Soar examined me with way-too-wise eyes. "Light's not some woman you fuck and walk away from. She's a keeper."

I scoffed. "I'm not interested in a mate."

Jackal leaned forward with a smile and eager eyes. "If you don't want her, would you have a problem with me pursuing her?"

My eyes flashed.

"That's what we thought. She's all yours, alpha," Jackal commented smugly.

I struggled to get myself under control. "All I care about right now is pack business," I remarked while coolly watching them. "Let's review what we know so everyone's on the same damn page."

Soar slid his finger over the tablet. The myriad of monitors flicked to life. My eyes narrowed on the streaming images from the crime scenes, autopsies, and copies of the reports appearing on the monitors.

"Here are the photos we got from our informants. Notice the heart is ripped out of every single body." Soar eyed us. "What's more puzzling is the hearts were not found on the scenes." He paused, scratching his head. "And the animal maul marks on the bodies . . . were definitely made by a shifter."

"Shifters don't take organs," I argued. "And if we did, what the fuck would we do with them? Our organs are useless once they leave the body." It was nature's way of ensuring the essence and power of Others remained within the body.

"That's exactly what I concluded, but someone is going to great lengths to frame shifters." Soar leaned back in his chair. "What's even stranger is the neighbors reportedly heard howling around the timeframe of the attacks. Some even said they saw wolves running in the street."

"What the fuck? Wolves running in the middle of Manhattan?" I ran my hands through my hair. "This shit is out of control. Whoever did this is going to pay for jeopardizing the peace treaty talks."

"Frankly, I don't think you have a chance in hell of getting the Others to the table now," Jackal interjected. "They're too riled up. Chatter on the network is going crazy. Wild speculation is running rampant, but the main theme is everyone thinks the stolen Credence client book is some type of Others hit list."

My jaw tensed. "Can this get any worse?"

"Oh, it has," Rip commented. "We've also picked up unusual chatter in the Others network about humans purchasing Others' hearts."

I sat straight up. I didn't like the sound of this at all. The few humans who knew of our existence had been trying to get their hands on Others' organs. They believed by implanting the organs into humans, they would somehow get the Others' strength and power. If the network chatter was true, it meant someone had figured out how to successfully harvest Others' organs.

"Rip, call Ben from the Riley pack. He might know what's going on." I paused. "A couple months ago, I got a strange call from a former colleague. He was frantic about a visit from a group of rich humans who said they were from a corporation called Swodah Unified. He said they were looking to purchase Others' organs. He told them it was impossible and not to come back. I gave the lead to Ben since he had been monitoring this group's activities for years. See if he has any new intelligence." I stared sharply at Jackal. "Find out the names of the humans who purchased the organs. We find the names, and it will lead us to who's behind the killings."

I scrutinized the images flashing on the monitors. "Stop." My eyes narrowed on the bodies of the two top enforcers from the Calum pride, Dimitri and Houston. "Soar, pull up the address on where the bodies were found." A map of the city flashed on the screen, with a big red dot pinpointing the locations of the bodies. "That's one block away from Redemption. Too much of a coincidence. Pull up the video surveillance we have on Redemption."

One of the first things I'd done when I took over as leader of the council was start secret video surveillance on Redemption, a restaurant owned by a vampire named Vivica and frequented by key players in the New York Others circle. I was more concerned with Reason's father, Oskar Orlov, who was also Vivica's close friend and leader of the only vampire coven in New York. He was the man I needed to keep tabs on as discreetly as possible.

"I swear, Bones, if you don't get out of my way, I'm going to punch you in the damn throat," Light yelled from outside the conference room's door. "And I don't give a crap about what Ryker said. I'm going in that damn room. Now move." The door opened, with Light standing in the doorway. "What is this?" She paraded into the conference room as Bones stood behind her with an apologetic look on his face.

My body stilled. "I thought I told you to wait outside with Bones. This is pack business."

Without pause, she stepped up to the bank of monitors that made up my wall and stared at the photos from the crime scenes, autopsies, and reports. "I'm not waiting outside with Bones," she responded sarcastically. "Besides, from the looks of these photos, this has everything to do with me, pack or not." She stood in front of the monitors, staring at the gruesome images without even flinching. "Detective Prick wasn't exaggerating. Their hearts really were removed from their bodies." She turned to scrutinize me. "Who would do some sick shit like this?"

"You are testing my damn patience, Light," I gritted out through clenched teeth.

She calmly sat down. "I'm not leaving, Ryker. I have as much to lose here as you."

Bones shut the door and sat down.

I surveyed her with hard eyes. "Whatever you see, whatever you hear cannot leave this fucking room, Light."

She stared at me with wide, clear eyes. "Trust me, alpha."

I nodded toward Soar. "Roll the video surveillance."

Anger simmered like a raging fire underneath the cool exterior of my alpha façade as I watched Noah step out of a black vehicle and stroll up to Dimitri and Houston. The men shook hands and then walked into Redemption.

"What the fuck? I thought Noah was in London," Rip barked.

I deliberately said nothing, letting the sound of silence speak volumes. There could only be one reason Noah had secretly crept back to New York to meet with the second-in-command of two of my strongest adversaries—betrayal.

"Enzo"—my eyes snapped to Rip—"go get him."

Light raised her hand. We all stared at her.

"Who the hell is Enzo?" she asked.

I answered with deadly calm, "Noah's cousin."

8

LIGHTNING

I watched with fascination as Ryker's pack sorted through the information and images without pause. For a pack of only five, they were efficient, tight, and ran like a damn well-oiled machine. But their personalities were as different as they came.

"How did you meet each other?" I asked.

They all glanced up, contemplating me like they'd forgotten I was even in the room.

I shrugged. "You seem like unlikely friends."

Jackal leaned back in his chair and smiled. "Soar, Rip, and I met in the military. We worked on some secret missions together. And we met the former cardiologist here"—Jackal nodded toward Ryker—"when he saved Rip's life." He rubbed his head. "Shit, Rip's heart had fucking stopped after he was injured during our last mission. Hell, we'd thought he was a goner."

"That's why we nicknamed him Rip—Rest in Peace," Soar injected. "When we got to the hospital, the doctor here brought him back to life. We've been friends ever since."

I watched as Ryker settled his sinewy six-foot-three frame into the comfortable-looking, straight-back chair while savoring a cigar.

Jackal smiled. "So it wasn't much of a decision when Ryker

asked us to come back to New York with him to rebuild his pack. He's our leader. We respect and trust him with our lives."

The door whipped open. Rip stood in the doorway with a shaking man in tow.

"Sit," Rip replied gruffly, shoving the man into a chair.

Ryker stood up, getting right to the point. "Did you know Noah was meeting with Dimitri and Houston?"

Enzo's eyes timidly flitted around. "What?"

"Did you know?" he asked again with more calmness than I'd thought he was capable of.

Enzo stared and then babbled, "Yeah. Yeah, I knew."

Soar and Rip snarled with looks of disappointment on their faces.

Enzo's eyes darted over to the door. "I told him I wanted nothing to do with it." He paused. "You don't understand. Noah's changed. He hasn't been the same since"—his eyes flew over to Ryker—"you made Knox your beta instead of him. He felt disgraced. You and he were childhood friends. He'd worked as an enforcer for the pack for years when your father was alpha. He'd earned that damn spot."

"And that's exactly why I didn't choose him. He was corrupted by the years he stood idly by as my father waged war after war with Others in his lust for power. All that doesn't matter. I'm the fucking alpha of this pack now, and I don't answer to anyone about the decisions I make," he growled menacingly.

Enzo cowered.

Claws emerged from Ryker's fingers. "I have one damn rule. Betrayal is not an option. You betray me, and I'll kill you. You tell Noah if he wants to challenge me, then bring it. Got it?"

Enzo acknowledged uneasily.

"Now get the fuck out."

Enzo scrambled out of the chair and exited.

Ryker looked at Soar and Jackal. "I want to know what the fuck Noah is up to. I know him. And right now, he's hiding like some damn coward. I want you to turn this city upside down. Do what you do best. Go find Noah and bring him to me. But I want him alive. I'm going to enjoy killing him myself. Go." He glared at Bones. "Contact Vivica. Tell her I changed my mind, and I will be attending her party tonight." Then he nodded over at Rip. "Call Oskar Orlov's people. I want a meeting with him tonight. Tell him we'll meet at Vivica's party."

They exited the office. I watched warily as Ryker tensely stared out the window, looking out at the Manhattan skyline.

"What about the Credence client list?" I asked loudly.

He didn't turn to look at me when he responded, "What about it?"

I marched over to him. "Why aren't you looking for the person who stole it?"

"Because I don't give a shit who stole it. My job is to protect you. I have bigger issues."

"Are you serious? Finding the person who stole it is the key to solving your issues."

He ignored me.

I rolled my eyes with disgust. "Okay, fuck it. So what now, Wolfie? Do we run through Manhattan, snarling, as we declare war on Noah?" I tapped my chin. "Because I can totally go for kicking his ass in a senseless war."

Ryker turned to stare at me with a stony face. "Do you think this is some joke? My pack is relying on me to lead them, to protect them. Now I'm on the verge of another damn pack war because some crazy fuck is out there, gutting Others—Others who are your clients—like lab experiments and framing shifters," he retorted.

He looked me up and down like I was some shit on the bottom of his designer shoes. "And I don't need some out-of-control party lush making fun of shit that her inebriated mind can never understand," he stated flatly.

I swallowed the hurt, raising my brows at his condescension. "Party lush?" My eyes narrowed. "Go fuck yourself, Ryker." My voice hitched, and I hated myself for it. I cleared my throat. "I am not stupid."

He gave me a look that said he didn't agree.

I gritted my teeth and worked on slowing my pulse. "I give up. You shifters are mindless fucks who don't give a shit about anything but yourselves."

"And what the hell does a hybrid fae witch know about shifters?" he sneered. "Oh, I forgot. You're a Credence, which makes you an expert on all things shifters. Or do you have daddy issues? Is your father a shifter? What did your idiotic fuck of a father do to make you so bitter against all shifters and men?"

I placed my hands on my hips. "I never knew my father." I pursed my lips. "If he's like most men and like you, he probably isn't worth shit. But for the record, between boozing it up," I spit sarcastically, "I've seen enough of the shifters' political bullshit to turn my damn stomach. Case in point, this fucking pack. Your father was a brutal fuck. You couldn't pick up the Others newspaper without reading about the bodies and packs he'd destroyed in his quest to remain the strongest New York pack."

His eyes turned icy. "I'm nothing like my father." His canines dropped and his claws extended from his fingers.

I pointedly looked at his claws. "Really?"

"I don't need this shit." He stalked over to the chair, tensely sitting down. His eyes hardened. "I turned my back on my father and this pack when I was eighteen because I was tired of my father leading the pack from one senseless war to another until the pack was almost destroyed. He didn't care about the members. He was obsessed with power, money, and winning. I'm trying to change this mess around, and now my fucking hands are being forced, dooming me to repeat the same stupid-ass mistakes every alpha in my family made." He leaned back with his eyes closed, as if he were trying to get himself under control, but it wasn't working. His claws were still extended, his breathing shallow.

I sighed, feeling stupid and childish. He was hurting. He was paying the price for his father's mistakes. It was something I could relate to, given what I now knew about my father. I hadn't thought first, as usual. His pack was his family, and like me, he was fiercely protective of them. Shit, if anyone even looked at Storm wrong, I would be ready to kick major ass.

In the blink of an eye, before I realized what I was doing, I walked over to him, straddled him, and cupped his face.

His sea-green eyes snapped open. "Light? What the hell are you doing?"

The deep timbre of his voice sent a shudder down my spine. *Damn, it was sexy.*

"I'm spiraling out of control. When I get like this, I'm dangerous. And nothing can calm my beast, except time to cool down."

I didn't move. Instead, I ran a finger across the scar on his left eyebrow. Strangely, he tenderly leaned his face into my hand, wrapping his arms around my back. I tried not to blink in shock. Dammit, he was turning out to be exactly the opposite of what I'd envisioned. Despite his steel demeanor, I sensed the passionate streak that ran through his core. He actually cared about his pack and Others. This wasn't what I'd imagined him to be as an alpha from a cold-blooded bloodline.

I ran my fingers across his well-groomed dark beard, enjoying the softness. He growled low and sensually. I felt the slight prick of his claws through my shirt, which normally would have sent me sprinting away, but there wasn't anything normal about this strange connection between us. Slowly, I felt his claws retract, and his blunt fingers caressed my back.

His full focus was on me, the attention giving me little tremors of awareness as we stared at each other, speechless, our faces mere inches apart.

Ryker leaned into my body and pressed his lips against mine before he sucked my tongue into his mouth. My tongue slid around the tip of his and then rubbed under it. My body pulsed with need, and every cell was focused on him. His hands slid up to my neck, possessively grabbing the back of my head, before he softly kissed my throat. The contradiction between the hardness of his grip on my hair and the gentleness of his kiss sent a shiver down my spine while my mind imagined all the other delicious things his mouth could do.

What would those big hands feel like on my body? My skin quivered at the idea.

I closed my eyes for a moment to rein in my wayward thoughts.

Ryker Alfero was trouble. I had known that from the minute I met him at the charity gala. He was the one man I couldn't lead around by his cock, the one man I would never be able to control with a glance or a few flirtatious yet snarky words. I could see it in his feral but gorgeous sea-green eyes. Nope. Ryker was a smoldering fire that would consume me.

And I'd been down that road before with Nolan. He had left me broken but taught me a good lesson—never confuse mind-blowing sex with trust. I'd allowed Nolan to exploit me while simultaneously giving away a piece of me that I'd had to fight to take back—control. And I was never relinquishing that ever again.

But sex? I wouldn't think twice about satisfying my curiosity about how good or bad the alpha was in bed.

"You're an enigma, alpha," I whispered while trailing my fingers across the snake tattoo on the right side of his neck before digging my hands into his short, jet-black hair.

His green eyes warmed as he smiled in a slow, sexy way, making every fiber of my being strain toward him, wanting to strip off his clothes and have my wicked way with him.

"There's no enigma. I'm an open book for the right woman who's willing to put in the work required." He grabbed my hand, kissing each of my fingers one by one.

I pulled my hand away and swallowed down the thick longing, forcing myself to think before I did something I knew I would regret, like throwing caution to the wind. Deep down inside, I knew I was already addicted to Ryker in a most troubling way.

Contrary to common sense, I leaned in, allowing my body to slightly graze his broad chest. "I'm definitely not that woman, alpha, because I'm not willing to put in the amount of work required."

"Well, that's a fucking shame." His strange green eyes narrowed. "I thought you would have been up for the challenge."

The door slammed open. Bones came bursting in with Jackal.

"Hey, we got a hit on the—" Jackal bellowed.

I slid off Ryker's lap, brushing my hair away from my eyes.

Jackal smiled smugly. "Are we interrupting something?"

"No," we both snapped simultaneously.

Bones shook his head. "*O-kay* . . ."

"What did you get a hit on?" Ryker asked.

I coughed nervously. Jackal and Bones looked from me to Ryker, relishing the moment.

"We confirmed the name of the company that's selling Others' hearts—Swodah Unified," Jackal muttered. "And yes, it's a shell company for the Shadows."

WITH DISINTEREST, I LOOKED THROUGH THE CAR WINDOW, trying hard not to jump every time Ryker's leg rubbed against mine. "So we're going to Vivica's party tonight?"

Ryker raised an eyebrow, looking at me like I'd lost my mind. "There is no *we*. I'm going. You're staying with Bones at my penthouse." He nodded toward Bones, who was driving through the city at a breakneck speed.

I scooted farther away from Ryker, smiling coolly. "No offense, but your people skills suck. You need me with you."

He scowled.

"Besides, you're wasting valuable time. You and I know as soon as you leave, I'll figure out a way to escape and go to the party anyway. Why don't you just take me to avoid all the unnecessary drama?"

"No."

"I already texted Reason. She's going to be there, along with her father."

He sharply looked at me.

I glared at him. "And no, I didn't tell her anything. But believe me; having me and her there will go a long way in smoothing the discussions," I whispered loudly.

Not that I wouldn't enjoy going to Vivica's notoriously elaborate kink party, but tonight, something was nagging at me. I needed to go there with Ryker. I sensed trouble, and even though he was a pain in the ass, I needed him alive—for now.

"I could handcuff you to the bed," he barked.

I turned my head, but not fast enough to hide my smile. "Tempting offer. But I also dated a cop. I know how to get out of cuffs . . . when I want to," I replied huskily.

He smiled at me. "Why the hell did I agree to protect you?"

I smiled back. "Because I'm beautiful and perky?"

"You are beautiful, but I don't know about perky."

Bones laughed. I frowned.

"Look, if you think I'm going to sit at your penthouse, twiddling my thumbs, you've got another thing coming." I sighed heavily. "Ryker . . ."

I touched his thigh. The muscle jumped under my caress. I quickly pulled my hand back.

"You and I need each other right now. I have as much to lose in this mess as you do. Why don't you let me help?" I smiled. "Besides, the faster we figure out this shit, the faster you can get rid of me." I wagged my brows.

"Now we're talking. An incentive," he grumbled. "I don't want any shit out of you tonight, Light. We go to the party; you stick by my side. And that is not negotiable."

I shot him a dirty look. "What's with this nonnegotiable bullshit? Everything is negotiable."

He growled impatiently.

I rolled my eyes. "Fine. I'll be a good little girl and stick by your side."

Bones scoffed at my statement.

"Quiet, Bones. No one asked for your opinion," I retorted.

My eyes narrowed when we pulled up to the block Ryker lived on—well, not lived on. He *owned* all the brownstones and the building that held his penthouse, among other apartments his enforcers lived in. I sat forward, curiously looking around, when the underground parking garage opened, allowing Bones to swiftly drive in before it closed smoothly behind us.

"Hey, Ryker, do you need me for the party tonight?" Bones asked with an overly eager look in his eyes.

"No. Jackal and Rip will go. You and Soar follow up on our leads," Ryker grumbled. Blowing out a breath and unbuckling his seat belt, he placed a hand on my shoulder. "Okay, here's the game plan. We're in and out. You go upstairs and get changed, and then we go." He sighed tiredly. "I'm not in the mood to play around."

"No dinner?" I frowned, looking down at my watch. "I'm starving. We eat first. Then we get ready to go. And *that's* not negotiable."

"Shit. It's been a long day. I'm used to skipping dinner sometimes," he commented before getting out of the car.

"No biggie. I'll make us something to eat, and then we'll go," I responded while following him.

He arched a brow. "You cook?" he asked gruffly, putting an arm around me, steering me toward the elevator and away from Bones's more-than-interested stare.

I cast a quick glance at Ryker, only to find he was watching me. "Of course I cook." My breath caught when I saw something flash in his eyes.

"Well, you don't have to worry about cooking. Rosa normally handles the cooking."

The elevator finally arrived, and I sauntered onto it. "Rosa?" I responded with a forced infusion of nonchalance.

He punched in a code, and the door closed. Feeling awkward about his lack of a response, I turned to him and stared.

He turned toward me, patiently watching me. "Rosa's my aunt."

I nodded, momentarily looking away, upset I'd let on that I even cared.

"You do know what type of clientele Redemption caters to?" His voice jarred me from my thoughts. His full focus was still on me.

What in the hell? I rolled my eyes. "Yes, everyone knows about Redemption, Ryker. It's the hottest sexcapade in town."

Redemption was an upscale restaurant known for its anything-goes vibe. Vivica, a former model who was also a vampire, owned the well-known private restaurant. It was more of a VIP restaurant with a long waiting list, patronized by the rich and famous Others and humans. The difference between Vivica's restaurant and other celebrity-frequented restaurants was, everyone who went there wanted their privacy because of the type of acts that took place there. Sexual acts were orchestrated on a stage for all to see while patrons ate and watched. Given proper motivation, they would have their own private show in their booths.

"Tonight is going to be a little different. She's throwing an intimate party for a few of her VIP vampire clients. The theme is going to be a little darker, giving her clients the opportunity to live out their fantasies." He paused. "To be seen, watched, and played."

I shrugged. "What's the big deal? She throws invite-only kink parties several times a year."

"This party is primarily for vampires to get blood from Others and humans who want to walk on the wild side and who like to be bitten and have sex," Ryker told me matter-of-factly.

"It's not my thing, but hey, live and let live I say." I stared at him. "Do you normally go to her kink parties?" I asked boldly. I couldn't imagine him ever letting a vampire bite him, but looks could be deceiving.

His nostrils flared slightly. "No. Vivica's kink parties are way too dark for my tastes." He ran a hand across my cheek. "I'm more into discreet play. What about you?" His steady gaze pinned me in place.

My stomach tightened as heat crawled through my body. I stared boldly at him. "I love to watch. But I reserve my naughty play for private." I finished breathlessly as my heart hammered like I'd been running a marathon.

I could feel my nipples poking against my silk blouse. The dampness in my panties intensified. Shit, I really needed to get off this elevator before I did something stupid, like unzip his pants and wrap my lips around his surging manhood.

❧ 9 ☙

RYKER

I FOUGHT to keep my mind off her intoxicating scent, but the honey-sweet bouquet of her wet sex filled the air like perfume. My wolf fought to get out. My hands fisted as I fought the beast with all my might. My wolf clawed my insides, and I bit my lower lip from the vicious pain.

My plan for a one-night stand with Light was turning into something more meaningful . . . deeper. I knew now she was the one I had been waiting for all my life. My beast had known it from the moment I met her. She was mine . . . my mate.

But Light wasn't ready for me. I could tell by the way she would try to stamp down her own arousal. She wasn't ready to give me what I needed—her trust, her heart, and her body. I could feel her distress from fighting her needs and emotions.

I reached forward, slamming my fist against the button, stopping the elevator.

"What the fuck?" Light's eyes widened in confusion.

Her words were lost as I took her wrists, putting her arms around my neck. Pushing her legs apart, I moved between them. Hand on her ass, I slid her closer until her mound rubbed against my throbbing erection. I pulled back, enjoying that her body quavered from my touch. I cupped her cheek before sucking on her lower lip, drawing it into my mouth, my tongue sliding across it. I enjoyed the lovely sweetness of her pouty lips. My beast rattled in his cage as I grabbed her close, swallowing her sighs and moans in my mouth. I was unrelenting, taking the kiss deeper.

❧ 10 ❧

LIGHTNING

I WAS TREMBLING ALL OVER. My hands dug into Ryker's wide shoulders so tightly that my fingers ached. I rocked against his muscled body, both shocked and excited at the hardness of his penis, which pushed into my stomach. His hand slipped beneath my blouse. I grabbed it while pulling my lips away.

I wasn't a prude. In fact, I loved sex, but after spending a lifetime picking and fucking all the wrong men, I'd decided months ago that celibacy was the only way to stop the vicious cycle—that and the fact that the empath madness had been getting worse with each man I slept with.

"This is not a good idea, alpha." I was surprised at the huskiness in my voice.

He rubbed his nose against the sensitive spot on my neck. "Why?"

"You know why. Because it will be messy and complicated, and I don't do messy and complicated."

He looked at me with a wolfish smile on his sexy lips, which made me take a step back with alarm. My clit thumped, and before I knew what was happening, he pressed his body against mine.

Ryker's tongue darted out and intimately caressed my neck

before he nipped it so hard that jolts went straight down to my pussy. My body wanted to do this, not worry about anything long term or the ripple effects it might have. But my mind rebelled.

I tried to step away from him, but he held me tight.

"I don't like to be touched," I hissed at him.

He watched me with delicious intensity, which immediately made me all hot and jittery.

"Really? Because it smells like you love my touch," he responded with an erotic swirl in his voice.

I was uncomfortable that he saw me too clearly. It was frightening how my body reacted with one look, one inflection in his voice. What was infuriating was he was right. I loved his touch. I loved it way too much, and that was the fucking problem.

No sex, I chanted over and over again.

I licked my lips as I examined his brooding dark looks, and all I could think about was how desperately I wanted to wrap my legs around his narrow waist and ride him like a stallion.

No, no, no. This would be a fucking mistake.

I knew deep in my gut that it would never be as simple as sex with Ryker. He would want more control . . . and wouldn't settle for less than my submission.

His phone rang, yanking me out of my near panic.

"Don't move," he growled low, reaching for his cell. "Yeah?" The fingers of his free hand caressed my throat and jaw as he stared at me. "I'll be there tonight," he drawled into the phone.

Like a coward, I jolted the button. The elevator began to ascend.

Ryker smirked. "Look, I'll call you back in a few minutes." He hung up, turning all his attention back to me. "I guess playtime is over," he stated with amusement.

I moved to the other end of the elevator, as if it changed the closeness of our proximity. "Playtime was a mistake, a mistake never to be repeated."

His eyes narrowed at my brutally cold detachment. I frantically pressed the button, as if it would make the elevator move faster.

"It's like that?" he murmured.

I swallowed hard. "Don't have a clue what you're talking about."

He shook his head. "I don't play games, darling. So if you want to act like what just happened didn't, I won't make it fucking easy. What we felt was special, but if you want to deny it because you're too fucking scared to explore it further, that's all on you, darling." The elevator opened, and he looked at me with a blank stare. "Follow me."

I glanced down at my hands. They were shaking, but not from fear. It was the first time I regretted my inability to form normal relationship attachments.

Without another word, we stepped directly into a grand foyer leading to a magnificent living room and dining room with floor-to-ceiling windows showcasing panoramic views of Central Park and the city. We walked into the luxurious penthouse. I followed him past an impressive collection of artwork into a large living room with a stunning raven-haired small woman sitting on the sofa, sipping a glass of red wine. Her eyes inquisitively lingered on me. Then she turned to Ryker.

My eyes narrowed when Ryker kissed her on the cheek.

"Rosa, whatever you cooked smells delicious."

Rosa affectionately patted his cheek. "Risotto with black truffles." Abruptly, she looked over at me with a ridiculously striking white smile, making her look even more gorgeous. "Ah, there she is . . . Lightning Credence. Get your beautiful ass over here." She patted the spot next to her.

The woman had used *beautiful* and *ass* in the same sentence. I instantly liked her.

"I don't mind if I do." In one smooth move, I sauntered over to the sofa, sitting down with a sigh.

Ryker's cell rang. He looked at it and said, "I need to take this. Rosa will show you around." He walked away without another word.

Rosa poured another glass of wine, handing it to me. "A messenger delivered your luggage. I had it placed in the room next to Ryker's." She warmly looked at me.

"Thank you." I took a sip of wine, interestedly staring right back at her.

Rosa took another sip of wine. "He's been waiting for a long time," she uttered. "And so have you."

"Waiting? Waiting for what?"

"For the one to fill the emptiness," she stated matter-of-factly.

I was rattled at the observation but tried to play it off. "No offense, but there is no emptiness for me, especially not any for your nephew to fill." I took a huge swallow of wine. "I saw Sophia, so I know how he fills his emptiness," I countered.

Rosa smiled quickly. "There was a time when he was wild and slept around a lot. But I haven't seen that guy since he came back to New York. Why do you think that is?"

I bit my lip. "Rosa, I can't say. I really don't know Ryker at all."

"He was waiting for you," Rosa stated as some sort of fact.

I silently glared at her. Rosa gave me another pointed look.

"Look, Rosa, I don't know where you're getting your information from, but you don't know me or why I'm here—"

She shooed me with her hand. "Ava explained everything."

My eyes widened. "You know my aunt?"

"And your mother. I've known them for years. I used to work for them before I found my mate. It was a long time ago, but true friendship never ends." She smiled.

I stared at Rosa. "Wow . . . just . . . Does Ryker know?"

She shrugged. "Of course. There was a time when my father kicked me out of the pack when I'd refused to accept a mating with a wolf-shifter from another pack. Your mother and aunt took me in and gave me a home without any strings attached. I started working for them because I wanted to. When I was financially set, I left, forging my own way, and I aimlessly traveled the world. Eventually, I found the love of my life—a human—and I settled down."

Her eyes saddened. "When he died, I drifted a little. I returned when Ryker came back to lead the pack. I still don't want anything to do with pack life, but I'm here to take care of my nephews as much as they will allow me." She smiled. "I always wanted children, and I can't wait to spoil theirs."

I looked at her with a new respect. "I see."

She pointedly looked at me. "Do you? He's a good man."

"Rosa . . . I'm dealing—"

"I know. But sometimes, if you opened up a little, you would be surprised at what you could find."

She set her glass down, standing up. Abruptly, she pulled me up, tugging me into a big bear hug. For a few seconds, I awkwardly stood there. The woman patiently waited for me to hug her back. Only then did she let me go.

She held my hands, warmly looking at me. "Now let's get Ryker. You need to eat before you get ready for Vivica's party."

I sharply looked at her. "How do you know that?"

Rosa winked at me. "I know more than you think, empath." She tried to give me an innocent look but failed.

I GRUMPILY LOOKED AROUND THE LUXURIOUS BEDROOM. I WAS annoyed that Ryker hadn't come out of his office.

Rosa and I had had a hilarious dinner where we ate too much food and drank way too much wine. Surprisingly, the girls' bonding session still hadn't ended, much to my enjoyment. I arched a brow, watching Rosa circle the bed, looking at the outfits I had laid out as potential picks.

She pointed to the skintight short, black dress. "I like this one. The more skin you show, the better." She saucily smiled at me. "It's what my ass of a nephew needs to see. Show him what he's missing, no?"

I wanted to giggle at the look on her face. Her annoyed voice mixed with an Italian accent was straight out of a cinematic movie. I strolled over to her, looking closely at her choice, as she swirled the wine in her glass.

I smirked at Rosa. "Woman, are you trying to get your nephew laid?"

Rosa sipped her wine with a wicked look. "Most definitely."

I shook my head. Rosa was absolutely crazy, and I loved it.

I took another sip of wine. "You know that's not going to happen, right?"

She smugly looked at me. "That's what Storm said, and now she's mated to my nephew, Knox." Her eyes narrowed. "You and Ryker will require harder work, but I'm willing to put in all the work required to make it happen."

I rolled my eyes. "Okay, um . . . good to know." I tiredly plopped down onto the chair. "Why don't you come with us tonight? You can party." I wiggled my brows. "And maybe get your kink on."

Rosa pursed her lips with distaste. "I'm open to a lot of things, but getting bitten and fucked by a vampire is not on my to-do list."

I laughed. "It's not on my list either, but I'm going. I love to watch kinky fuckery."

"What a bad girl! It's going to be fun watching you take down Ryker like a deer." She pushed me toward the bathroom. "Go take a shower. We need to get you all hot and bothered. It's time to show my Ryker what he's missing."

"I'm surrounded by people as crazy as me. This is not a good thing," I mumbled.

RYKER

I SAT IN THE BACKSEAT, waiting impatiently for Light to come down. Jackal and Rip sat up front, displeased about attending Vivica's party. They both hated vampires. I wasn't partial to vampires myself, but Oskar Orlov had agreed to meet me at the party. And I needed to get the peace treaty talks back on track. Plus, I had to find out what the cold bastard knew about the Shadows.

Jackal glanced at his watch. "It's eleven o'clock. Where is she?"

"What's up with the time thing?" Rip replied calmly.

"It's late. It's bad enough that I have to go to this damn party."

Rip glanced at me. "He's so fucking uptight."

"Shut the fuck up, Rip," Jackal snapped.

I shook my head as I texted Soar the leads I wanted Soar to follow up on. I didn't want to talk about Light right now. She was starting to be a damn pain in the ass. In fact, I wouldn't even be taking her to the party if she hadn't stubbornly pushed to go. She was right. If I left her here with Bones, she would only figure out a way to manipulate him and escape to the party anyway.

The last thing I needed right now was for her to be roaming

around Manhattan, open game for whoever had a contract on her and her family. I knew what the real problem was. For the first time in my life, I'd met a woman who didn't even want to give me a chance. When I touched her, she'd yield beautifully, even when her reaction confused the shit out of her. Everything about Light intrigued me—her stubbornness, her intelligence, and her curvy body. But the choice to let me in, to trust me, had to be hers, up until she handed the right to me.

The elevator opened, and Light strutted out into the garage. I stared. How could I not? Light was a visual stunner. She wore her jet-black hair loose and straight with a hint of curl around the ends. Her skintight black mini dress slid over her curves like it had been designed solely for her. Its hemline stopped several inches above her knees and allowed glimpses of skin.

Part smolder, part fury, she walked over to the vehicle. Light exuded a hip-thrusting sensuality that would intimidate most men . . . but I wasn't most men. A voluptuous five feet nine, she stepped lively in a pair of thigh-high, peep-toe boots, which made my fingers clench, wanting her unabashedly curvaceous body.

Rip scrambled out with a look of admiration stuck on his face before opening the door.

I frowned when I realized it had been hours since I'd last seen her. My jaw tightened. I'd actually missed her annoying ass.

"Let's get this party started, shifters!" she yelled while sliding into the backseat. She smiled, locking eyes with me.

Everyone was silent until Jackal cleared his throat. "Um . . . are we ready to go?"

Light gave me a sexy smile. "Get that look off your face, Wolfie."

"What look?"

"The one telling me you wouldn't mind bending me over your knees and spanking my ass like I've been a bad girl." She slowly crossed her legs.

An image of those sexy legs wrapped around my waist while I

pumped her hard and fast flashed through my head. I was seconds from coming in my pants like an uncontrolled teenager.

I was starting to love this woman. "And are you a bad girl?"

She winked at me. "The baddest girl you'll ever know, Wolfie."

I silently cursed as I thought of the million ways I'd like to find out how bad she really was.

Light was tormenting me. Whether it was intentional or not, she was provoking me. And until I was buried deep inside her, there would be no peace for me.

"You really need to stop calling me Wolfie."

❦ 12 ❦

LIGHTNING

I COULD FEEL the heat of Ryker's stare as we pulled up to Redemption. His physical magnetism was palpable. I calmed my breathing as I glanced over at him. He had turned toward me and was sitting, patiently watching me.

Shit, no man should exude so much sex appeal. His jet-black hair kissed his collar. His rich beard added a hint of roughness to his lean, hard face. He wore tailored black slacks, and a black shirt outlined his hard muscles. Ryker was dark, deadly, and absolutely yummy. And he was trouble.

Right now, all I could think about was how beautiful he would be completely nude. My body pulsed with need, but I could resist my attraction to him for only so long. Months of denying sex was coming back to bite me on the ass. Now, my defenses were down.

"Having second thoughts, darling?" His green eyes flashed. There was humor but steel underneath as he watched me, as if he knew how close I was to laying myself at his feet and calling him Sir.

I lifted my chin. "None."

He was enjoying my struggle. "It's your call, darling. Let me know when you're ready to submit." He was all but laughing at me as his eyes glinted. Breaking contact with me, he opened the car door. "Let's do it," he ordered, getting out of the vehicle.

After pulling me out, Rip and Jackal followed out of the car.

I stared curiously at the people walking up to the entrance blocked by several huge security guards.

A well-toned young man dressed in a well-cut suit greeted us with a cool smile. "Welcome, Alfero," he announced, stepping out of the way as one of the guards opened the door.

I didn't flinch when Ryker wrapped a protective arm around me, tucking me into his side. He was so big; I felt tiny next to him. He led me through the entry and into a huge room crowded with people. The heavy pounding of the music reverberated throughout the dimly lit room, setting the mood for the anything-goes vibe.

My eyes widened as I looked around. The expensively designed restaurant had been transformed into a club on the entire first floor. Rich fabric draped across the ceiling. Victorian-style birdcages with naked women dancing inside were tucked into the corners of the room. I almost giggled at the coy, cheeky aura of some of the women swinging back and forth as they sat on their perches like birds. I was like a kid in a candy shop. I was mesmerized by more women hanging from ropes attached to the ceiling, twisting like a washing machine, before they intertwined and rotated like helicopter blades with each other.

I checked out the room. My gaze stopped at a couple in the corner. The huge man pulled a barely dressed woman to him. He tangled his hands in her hair and tipped her head back to take her lips. He thoroughly kissed her before pulling back with his canines glinting. I blinked and then watched with fascination as he kissed her neck and bit down. The woman's eyes glazed over with ecstasy.

"This place is fucking amazing," I whispered under my breath.

The perimeter of the dance floor had several booths with high backs and wide sides facing away from the area where the guests could dance, obstructing the view of any possible voyeurs. Suddenly, some of the booths swung to face the dance floor, giving me a full view of the guests attired in extremely suggestive clothing—from latex to corsets to skintight leather. My curiosity was piqued when I saw one man dressed only in tight leather pants, kneeling beside a woman who wore a latex dress. His fangs sparkled as he bit the woman's extended wrist.

Damn, watching the sexual acts was getting me overheated. The scent of sex permeated the air around us. My nipples hardened. A couple brushed past us, the woman leading a man with a leash strung to a collar around his neck.

Ryker looked at me with a hint of laughter in his eyes before nodding over to the booths. "The guests control the booths, allowing us to watch." Amusement sparkled in his eyes as he pulled me close, running a finger down my cheek. "Are you rethinking your stance on public play?" he asked with a sensual tinge to his voice.

Something inside me tightened at his words. "Depends on my motivation." I reached up, dragging my fingers through his hair. "Do you want to be my motivation, alpha?"

The live band kicked off a sultry rock song. Undulating bodies filled the dance floor, writhing and grinding to the music. Ryker slipped his fingers under the edge of my dress, caressing my ass. His eyes were intent on my face, as if he could read my reactions.

My head fell against his chest.

"No, darling. I need to see those beautiful eyes." He grabbed the back of my hair, tilting my face to look at him before bringing his mouth down on mine. His lips were unyielding, clever, teasing a response from me.

A stinging nip of his canines made me open my mouth, and he plunged in, his tongue stroking mine. My clit clenched, and everything inside me shattered with his kiss. My hands curled around his muscular forearms as a searing need burned between my legs.

He had me wrapped around his finger, and he knew it. He grabbed my wrists, tugging my arms around his neck. Shoving my legs apart, he stepped between them. Digits on my ass, he glided me nearer until my throbbing, moist sex caressed against his thick, hot erection. He took the kiss deeper, his hold unrelenting. I shook all over. My fingers tightly burrowed into his broad shoulders, leaving nail marks on his skin.

He pulled back. "Is that enough motivation?" he asked with a husky voice.

"Definitely," I whispered.

I wanted him more than my next breath. This was about to go down—right here, right now. And I didn't give a shit about the repercussions.

Caressing my cheek, he tugged on my lower lip, pulling it into his mouth, his tongue sliding across it. And when he released me, a wicked smile told me he wanted me in no uncertain terms.

Someone coughed, gently breaking our intimate moment. We both looked over, perplexed to see a lean, muscular man looking at us.

"Alfero, welcome. I'm Jacque, Mistress Vivica's assistant," he murmured. "She would have greeted you herself, but she's occupied at the moment." He nodded over to a booth with two somber-looking men standing guard.

My mouth fell open at the sight of a blond woman draped over Vivica while Vivica sucked blood from the woman's wrist. Vivica looked up, showing us her canines in a sexy smile.

Ryker acknowledged her with a curt nod while safely tucking me against his side. Rip and Jackal flanked us, so three menacing large wolves effectively surrounded me.

"Vivica reserved a private booth for you, of course." Jacque stole a glance at me before turning away. "Please, this way."

I felt the change in Ryker's attitude as we made our way through the crowd of half-naked gyrating bodies. It was cold and deadly. If there had been a doubt in my mind of the dangerous beast he truly was, it was quickly erased. Even Jackal's and Rip's lips were drawn tight in serious expressions, projecting their menacing dominance.

Spotting Reason, I stopped, squeezing Ryker's arm. "I see Reason. I'll meet you over at our booth."

Ryker simply nodded at Jackal. "Take care of her."

Jackal nodded back before following me across the dance floor.

"Hey, sweetie." I embraced Reason in a tight hug.

Jackal came up behind me, no doubt keeping watch.

I pulled back with a raised brow. "The stuff going on here is kinky, even for me."

"What can I say? My aunt loves to do it up kinky style," Reason ranted with a devilish grin.

I gasped at a naked woman strapped to a wooden X on the wall. The sight of the woman tied there, her legs open and breasts hanging free, fascinated me.

I shook my head and stared at Reason. "Aunt?"

She shrugged. "Not related, but she's been Father's close friend for so long that she's come to be a part of my dysfunctional family."

I winked at her. "So she's the freaky aunt?"

"What can I say? Freakiness runs in the family." Reason flashed her exposed canines at Jackal. "Hey, Jackal." She smiled flirtatiously. "Would you like to take a walk on the vampire side and find out how freaky I can be?"

Jackal snorted. "Not on your life, vampire."

Reason looked him up and down with interest. "You know what they say. Once you go vampire, you never go back."

"I don't care what they say, sweetie. It ain't happening," he commented.

Reason blew a kiss at him before tossing her long auburn hair over her shoulders.

I laughed, loving Reason's attempt at foreplay. "Is there something I'm missing between you two lovebirds?"

"He's playing hard to get," Reason whispered loudly. "Don't think I haven't seen you checking out my ass." She impishly stared at him while shaking her hips and bottom in a twisting manner.

"Twerk it!" I high-fived Reason and then smiled at Jackal. "Now where else would you see a hybrid vampire twerking but here, in this den of sin?"

Jackal shook his head, his lips curling up into a smile.

Reason bit her lip. "Ah, there it is—that sexy smile that drives me crazy."

I smiled at her. The fun Reason was back with a vengeance, or maybe years of being celibate was finally catching up with her. Being cock-deprived for a year could make anyone stir-crazy. I'd never seen her so . . . giddy. I arched a brow. That could only mean one thing. She was really into Jackal. Shit, I didn't blame her. He was swoon-worthy gorgeous, but clearly, he wasn't into vampires.

"One minute, Jackal." I pulled her farther away from his hearing.

Reason grabbed my hips and swayed to the heavy beat of the music.

"Uh, Reason, you're making me nervous."

Reason stopped dancing, giving me a playful pout.

"Are you really going after Jackal?"

She waved at someone before staring at me. "No. I was fucking with him. He's hot and all, but I don't need to work that hard to get laid." She twirled her hair, staring at him. "But the sex with him would no doubt be fucking amazing."

"Say no to shifters, okay?" I grabbed her hand, diverting her stare away from Jackal.

Clearly, the men of the Alfero pack were sending everyone I knew, including me, into some crazy, lustful I-want-to-fuck-a-shifter-today frenzy.

"Really? You're casting judgment on me?" Reason rolled her

eyes. "And don't think I didn't see you dry-humping Ryker in the middle of the dance floor."

"It wasn't dry-humping. It was foreplay," I commented, when something caught my eye.

Ryker was holding court like a rock star as women gyrated suggestively, giving him his own private strip show. As if he felt my glare, he turned and cockily winked at me.

"So how is it going with the alpha?" Reason whispered in my ear.

Reluctantly, I broke eye contact with him, staring at her. "Horrible." I sighed heavily. "The man is a walking vibrator."

"Have you thought that he could be the one?"

I scoffed. "Oh, he's the one all right, the one capable of making me lose my damn mind."

"I'm serious."

I shrugged. "So am I. I gave up on that dream months ago. There is no Bringer of Death who's going to save the day."

Like a moth to a flame, my eyes drifted back to Ryker and a woman who had finagled herself into his booth, all the while flashing her canines and fake boobs in his face. Ryker stared at her with disinterest, but before I knew what I was doing, I walked away from Reason and moved through the sea of patrons like a woman on a mission.

My steps faltered when I saw a naked woman facing a wall, hanging from shackled wrists. A tall, muscular man stood behind her with a look of pure joy on his face. With a whooshing sound, he smacked the woman's ass.

Holy shit!

I shook my head and walked away, pushing at people as I bulldozed through the crowd to Ryker.

"I'm your girl, baby!" the woman told Ryker with an intensely sensual look.

"Sorry, girlie. I belong to him," I blurted like a nut. "I mean, this one is mine. So up you go, and get to stepping." I gestured for her to rise and exit left.

She gave me a hard stare, and even though she had the appearance of a woman who wanted to bite, chew, stab, and choke me, I didn't flinch.

She ignored me and stared at Ryker. "So . . . does she belong to you, shifter?"

Ryker's eyes narrowed on me before he pulled me onto his lap. He stroked the underside of my breast, his thumb rubbing the nipple. I felt the flare of warmth between my legs, but I was having none of it.

"Oh no, you don't." I yanked on his hand with no success.

"Now don't be rude. The vampire asked a question. Do you belong to me?" he murmured.

I froze, realizing his words of possession excited me. I wanted so badly to belong to him.

"Let's see, shall we?" he commented.

With a peeved sigh, I tilted my head up.

Grabbing the back of my head, he teasingly brushed his lips against mine, like he was discovering me for the first time. He took the kiss deeper, opening my lips with his own, coaxing me into responding. Under his slow assault, my mouth softened. Still deeper, he invaded my mouth, taking sweet control. My fingers tightened around his hand, so he tightened his fingers around my breast. Heat kissed my pussy, and when he sucked my tongue into his mouth, I moaned, feeling dizzy from lust.

His tongue dipped between the seam of my lips before he said, "Yes, she does belong to me."

He stared at me with an unwavering intensity as I licked my lips, still tasting him all over them.

"Damn. That was a fucking good kiss, alpha."

The woman looked at us, perturbed. "Lucky her," she spouted before sliding out of the booth and walking away.

My heart raced. *Shit. What the hell did I do?*

I tried to scramble off his lap, but he placed a hand on my thigh and gently squeezed. I looked up at him, noticing his face had softened. God, this man was killing me inside. Everything about him intrigued me, worried me, and made me want him even more.

I grabbed his glass of scotch, taking a nervous sip. My mind was contemplating on a strategy to exit left before I got myself further down the rabbit hole.

Ryker glanced over at Jackal and Rip and then back at me. "So, darling, what are you going to do now? Slink off and pretend this never happened?"

I nearly choked on the scotch. *What the hell?* "Whatever do you mean, Wolfie?" I batted my eyelashes at him. "I saw vamp girl bothering you, and I came to help. It was community service."

"Community service, huh?" Ryker inquired in an authoritative tone.

"Exactly." I felt my voice escalate.

Ryker wrapped a hand around my wrist. His eyes locked on mine in a passionate stare before they fell to my lips.

Damn, why do I want this man so badly?

Our connection was broken by someone clearing his throat.

It was the man who had greeted us at the door. "Mr. Orlov is ready to meet with you."

I glanced over at the man, trying to pull my hand away from Ryker, but he guided my palm onto his thigh. My eyes snapped back to him.

"We'll be there in a minute," he responded without breaking our eye contact.

I swallowed anxiously when I felt the soft slide of our connection grounding me to him. It was as if my physical touch against his thigh ramped up our strange connection. This was dangerous. All I could think about was him and how my feelings for him were spiraling out of control.

Is this physical attraction or something else?

I couldn't tell anymore, and it scared the living shit out of me.

My thoughts were interrupted by Rip's voice.

"Uh, Ryker, we really should go if we want this meeting to happen."

Ryker pushed me to my feet, wrapping an arm around me as my knees buckled. He ran his hands down my ass, squeezing each cheek, before slowly pulling down my dress.

"To be continued," he murmured, still stroking my ass.

My back stiffened as I tried to move away. "There is no *to be continued.*"

Without saying another word, he efficiently ushered me through the club and into the darkened lobby. The farther we walked, the more the lighting changed, growing ominous. At the end of the passageway was an emergency exit door, and to our right were open double doors leading into a dimly lit room. My eyes instantly went to Vivica, who was whispering urgently to Oskar, but she stopped when her eyes snapped toward us with interest. Two men nearby flanked her sides, closing ranks.

Oskar frigidly looked at Ryker before slightly bowing his head, never taking his eyes off mine. "How lovely to see you again, Light." He offered me his hand.

I smiled.

Oskar Orlov, Reason's father, was as debonair as usual. His perfectly styled hair accentuated his handsome good looks and lithe muscular body.

I stepped forward to take his hand. Ryker wrapped an arm around me, tucking me into his side.

I shot him an annoyed glare. "What?"

Ryker gave me a stern look. "No," he dictated.

Jackal and Rip moved protectively behind me.

I stared at him, knowing I had a couple choices—make a scene or respect his authority in front of Oskar and Vivica. I knew how important the power structure was among Others, so I opted to give Ryker a pass in the presence of company. The minute we stepped out of this room, I was going to set some things straight with the alpha.

Oskar turned a hard stare on Ryker. "It seems the alpha does not trust me with you."

A tired sigh escaped my lips. Any minute now, they were going to whip out their penises and start marking their territory.

Heads snapped toward the door when Reason burst into the room like the hounds of hell were nipping at her heels.

Oskar looked at her with warm eyes, opening his arms. "Ah, there's my little girl."

Reason stepped into his embrace. "Cut it out. I'm not little. I'm twenty-three."

He smiled indulgently. "A mere baby for a vampire, yes?"

Reason pulled back, frowning at him. "Never mind that, Dad. Why did you tell Stefan I was coming here tonight?"

Oskar frowned, baring his canines. "Because it's time to get familiar with your future consort."

Reason snorted. "That is never going to happen, so you can stop meddling in my love life, Father."

Vivica loudly cleared her throat. "Oskar? Please, not this again. She refuses to accept him, so leave it alone." She smiled at Reason. "How about a little acknowledgment of your aunt?" She moved forward, and the two men held her back, menacingly looking at Ryker, Rip, and Jackal. "Stop it." She swatted them. "What's wrong with you? You know Ryker."

One of the men jabbered, "It's the other two we're worried about."

My eyes widened at the drama unfolding.

Vivica winked at me. "Consorts—can't live with them; can't live without them." She pointedly looked at them before pushing past them and walking over to Reason to hug her. "You're working too hard, darling. You need to come to Redemption more often. You're due for a sound paddling. And I have the perfect Dominant who will break your ridiculous dry spell."

Jackal growled with displeasure.

Vivica looked at him with interest and then back at Reason. "Is the wolf-shifter yours?"

Reason's shoulders stiffened. "Nope. He's not interested in vampires."

"Well, that's a shame," she drawled.

Oskar looked at Jackal with aversion. "He should be so lucky to be in your presence. He's a wolf-shifter. You're a blueblood vampire. He's not worth your time."

Ryker widened his stance, staring menacingly at Oskar. "I'm going to forgive your insolence because I don't feel like getting my clothes dirty by kicking your ass."

Oskar's enforcers stepped forward at the same time Jackal and Rip advanced. Everyone around me stiffened, and an uncomfortable hush fell upon us.

I placed a gentle hand on Ryker's arm. "Can we do this without getting blood all over my designer dress?"

Ryker tilted his head as he considered me before nodding at Jackal and Rip. They walked backward. Reason gave her father an exasperated glare. He nodded stiffly to his enforcers. They also took a step back.

"I don't have time for this!" Oskar elucidated with an air of arrogance.

"Make time," Ryker drawled, his low tone emanating anger. "We have business we need to deal with."

"There is no *we*, shifter. My second-in-command has been slaughtered by your kind. And we are now on the verge of a vampire-shifter war." Oskar tilted his head. "I agreed to this meeting only to appease my curiosity."

Vivica scoffed.

"And because Vivica asked me to hear you out," Oskar said.

I didn't like this at all. My hand instinctively went to Ryker's back. I could feel his muscles bunch. He was pissed, but his face remained calm. The air stilled.

"We both know a war will not be good for any of us. Our numbers are already thin. We can't afford to lose any more vampires or shifters."

Oskar frowned. "And what do you plan to do to avoid the inevitable, bearer of the Sword of Souls?"

"I don't have time for bullshit, Oskar," Ryker told him with a tic in his jaw. "You and I know your coven is in disarray. If it weren't, Dimitri wouldn't have met with Houston and Noah behind your back."

They tensely stared at each other. The silence went on for so long that I forced myself not to shift anxiously.

"There are issues I'm currently resolving." Oskar's voice held an edge of rage, yet his demeanor was controlled.

"So we agree that the deaths of Dimitri, Houston, and the two shifters were not a coincidence," Ryker demanded brusquely. "Something's going on. And if we don't figure out what, we're not going to survive the week. Someone's trying to send our world spiraling toward war. Now, I need you to tell me what you know about the Shadows."

Oskar considered Ryker for a second. "They're a group of filthy warlocks who have been buying up property in Manhattan," he spit out. "I thought nothing of it until some of their members started visiting my clubs, asking a lot of detailed questions."

I stood quietly, but inside, I was seething.

"Questions about what?" Ryker inquired in an authoritative tone.

"About the peace treaty negotiations," Oskar answered.

"Do you know anything regarding the recent chatter about humans looking for Others' organs?"

Oskar shrugged. "Yes. But you and I know, it's not as simple as taking our organs or blood and becoming a shifter or vampire. If that were the case, we would all be extinct by now. Once our organs leave our bodies, they die."

"What if they figured out how to bypass that?" Ryker asked.

Vivica laughed. "Impossible."

"Not anymore," Jackal commented. "I have it from a good source that the Shadows have figured out how to harvest Others' organs. It won't make the organ recipient an Other, but it will significantly extend their life. It's like the holy grail, the equivalent of the fountain of youth for humans."

Vivica stared, dumbfounded. "They'll hunt Others like animals."

"They've already started," Ryker stated dryly. "Now the Shadows are everyone's problem." He stared at Oskar.

"Apparently," Oskar replied. "Let me call my contacts. They can help us."

My mind was reeling. I didn't know how much I should reveal about my link to the Shadows. *What would Ryker do?* I discreetly pulled out my cell, texted *9-1-1* to Mom, and wiped the sweat glistening on my forehead.

Ryker wrapped his arm around me. "Is everything all right?"
Damn his shifter senses.

He could probably smell the anxiety seeping out from my pores. I didn't want to lie. I knew telling him the truth would open a whole can of whoop-ass I wasn't prepared to deal with.

"I . . . uh . . . well . . ." My eyebrows rose as I slightly stepped away. "Shit . . . maybe we should . . ." I sighed when my cell rang. "Sorry, I need to take this."

My eyes darted toward the door, and I half-stepped toward it. Ryker grabbed my wrist.

"Are you sure everything is all right?" he hissed.

I looked deliberately at his hand. "Yep, pretty sure."

He grudgingly released me, nodding at Rip to go with me.

"No. I need a minute to take this call in private. I'll stay right outside this room. I promise." I sighed with relief when Ryker reluctantly conceded.

I walked out of the room, letting the darkness of the passageway shroud me.

"Hey, Mom?" I whispered. The cell crackled. "Great." I warily looked at the door before creeping farther down the passageway. "Mom?"

"Where are you, Light? The reception is shitty."

"Redemption . . ." I seethed. My hand clenched at my side.

"What are you doing there? Is Ryker with you?"

I could hear the anxiety in her voice, but right now, there were bigger problems.

"Ryker is meeting with Oskar. Look, we've got some issues here. They've figured out the Shadows are behind the killings."

Silence filled the air.

"Hold on. Let me put you on speaker." There was a beat of silence. "Okay, Ava's here. So the Shadows are behind the killings . . ."

"Fuck! I'm going to need a glass of wine for this," Aunt Ava snapped.

My hands started shaking. "The Shadows are selling Others' organs." My teeth gritted. "Look, I don't feel comfortable with not telling Ryker the truth about me. They're going to dig, Mom. And there's no doubt in my mind he will find out. I think I should tell him." I wasn't at ease with lying. It wasn't in my DNA. Right off the bat, I would say what I felt. There were no games with me, but now, it was as if I were being sucked into some shit I wanted nothing to do with.

"Listen to me. You cannot tell him."

"The hell I can't. We can trust him. If we couldn't, why would you have trusted him to protect me?" Now I was royally pissed.

"I'm not telling you not to. I'm saying, Redemption is not the place to do it. Wait until you get back to his place and then tell him," Mom commented.

A cold breeze brushed my neck. My eyes suspiciously darted around.

"Good. I've got to go. This passageway is creeping me the hell out. I'll call you when I tell him." I disconnected.

The hairs on the back of my neck stood up, as if someone were watching me. A chill ran through me. Maybe it was a bad idea to leave Ryker's protection.

I watched with disbelief and then horror as the emergency exit door at the end of the passageway flew open and men dressed in black stormed through it. I didn't think. I spun on my heel and ran before I felt the yank on my hair, slamming me against a marshmallow-soft body. I tried to scream, but a hand cupped my mouth as I kicked and clawed at the person dragging me toward the exit.

The other man with mousy-brown hair kept his eyes nervously darting around as he shuffled toward the exit. "Hurry up," he murmured. "And keep her quiet."

Oh my God. They're going to kill me. This is it. This is how I'm going to die.

I struggled harder, knowing full well if they got me out of Redemption, I would be fucked. The sharp edge of something cold was pressed against my throat.

I gagged at the smell of sour breath as the man holding me said against my ear, "I'll cut you like a fucking pig if you don't calm the hell down."

I flinched at the sting of the knife as he pressed it against my neck. My body tightened. There was no doubt in my mind that he would cut me right here.

From the darkness, a man uttered, "Let her go."

The man clutching me pinned me against his body. "Who's there?"

I stared in fascination when a man who appeared to be in his fifties emerged from the shadows, looking like an older version of James Bond, gray but still dangerous.

"Raphael," the brown-haired man hissed. "Your father knew the news of your daughter being in danger would finally bring you crawling out of your hole."

Raphael? This man is my father? The rush of adrenaline passed through my bloodstream.

"Rick and Barnes, why doesn't it surprise me that he's still using you two asses as his favorite errand boys?" Raphael answered, his voice easy and slightly bored. "Now go back and tell my father I'll never let him have her."

Seconds passed in silence before Barnes stammered, "Fuck you. You're a traitor to your kind."

Bam.

Raphael swooped forward with inhuman speed and punched Barnes, sending him crashing against the wall.

Ryker came crashing out of the room where he was meeting with Oskar and into the passageway, looking ominous and deadly. "Let her go." He pulled out a gun, aiming at Rick.

Rick swung around, using me as a shield.

"Rick, shit's not worth it," Barnes stuttered.

"He'll kill us if we show up without her!" Rick yelled, pressing the knife against my throat.

I flinched when the knife sliced me.

"And I'll kill you if you don't let her go," Ryker responded slowly and almost lazy-sounding.

Rick dragged me toward the exit. He stopped short when he saw Rip and Jackal blocking the exit with guns drawn. He was trapped.

Ryker stepped forward.

"This has nothing to do with you, wolf. Tell your men to step aside." Rick viciously sliced my arm.

I gritted my teeth. "Guys, he's not fucking joking here."

"This will not end well, Rick. Let her go," Raphael snapped.

Ryker glared at Raphael. "Who the fuck are you?"

Raphael ignored him, looking at Barnes and Rick with contempt. "For the life of me, I can't figure out why my father still has you dumbasses around."

Ryker's lips pulled back in a snarl, and I blinked at the length of his canines. "Let her go, and when I kill you, I'll make sure I won't make you suffer . . . much."

Barnes fidgeted nervously.

Rick scoffed, "If I go . . . she goes."

"Oh, to hell with this." I back-kicked him in the knee—hard.

Rick groaned, "Fuck," doubling over.

Turning around, I brought my knee up, connecting it with his face.

"Light, move!" Ryker snapped.

Rick was getting up. I dropped to the floor, getting the hell out of the way, as Ryker took the shot. Rick crumpled to the floor, dead, steps in front of me. Barnes sprinted to the exit. Rip intercepted him, easily snapping his neck. I flinched at the sheer brutality as Barnes landed with a dull thud onto the floor.

Raphael coldly looked on when Ryker pulled me to my feet. He gave me a light push, motioning me to move behind him, while pointing his gun at Raphael.

Raphael was either crazy or stupid, because he didn't move. He looked at me with a slight smile. "I've been waiting a long time to formally meet you, Light."

"Who the hell are you?" Ryker asked immediately.

I moved from behind Ryker.

His arm wrapped around me, pulling me to his side. "Light?"

"He's my father," I retorted easily, my voice belying the tension in my body.

Raphael nodded. "I am." His voice was strained. "Are you okay?" He reached forward to touch me.

I indignantly pulled away. I didn't want to be touched by him.

His hands dropped to his sides and tightened. He looked at Ryker, and his eyes flashed angrily. "Why did you bring her here? She was safer with Lia and Ava. They hid her for twenty-three years. Why isn't she with them?"

My heart pounded in my throat as Ryker furiously looked at me.

"What is he talking about?" Ryker asked me.

I nervously licked my lips when I noticed the crowd gathering around us in the passageway, curiously looking on. "We need to talk in private."

He snarled and looked over at Raphael. "Who are Lia and Ava hiding Light from?"

Raphael stared into space, as if listening to something. "More Shadows are coming. You have to get her out of here."

Ryker nodded at Oskar and his enforcers. "We need some privacy."

"We'll make sure to clean up the bodies," Oskar replied curtly before he and his enforcers slid back into the party.

Raphael anxiously looked around. "We don't have time for this."

"I'm not going anywhere until I know the truth," Ryker countered.

Raphael frowned at me. "Why didn't you tell him?"

I shrugged.

Raphael shook his head at me with disapproval before he continued. "My father is the leader of the Shadows. And he wants Light to help him complete a dream the Shadows have been trying to fulfill for centuries—to create a new race of Fae to destroy the Others."

Ryker's gaze fell to me and then went back to Raphael. "They're behind the recent deaths?"

"Can't say for sure, but if my father has anything to do with it, believe me, it can't be good." He worriedly looked at me. "Now, you have to go. Knowing my father, he's probably sent more of his minions to get her."

Ryker's lip curled upward, but he didn't protest. What he did next was a thousand times worse. "Rip, Jackal, I need some time to cool off. Make sure Light gets home safely." He shoved me toward them, storming away from me.

❧ 13 ☙

LIGHTNING

Ryker was pissed. But what hurt me the most was when he'd walked away without a backward glance. I was crushed. I would have felt better if he had yelled or snarled, but he hadn't. I should have told him the truth. To make matters worse, he hadn't even driven back to his penthouse with us. No, I'd had to suffer through the utter silence and accusing looks Rip and Jackal had given me all the way back to the penthouse.

Great. Now, I'm enemy number one.

I stepped out of the glass-enclosed walk-in shower, wrapping a big, fluffy towel around me. I sighed as I leaned against the marble bathroom vanity, looking at the already healing cuts on my body. Shit, this wasn't normal. I wasn't normal. I clenched my fist. I was a freak of nature like my father—no, not father. He was my sperm donor.

Angrily, I pushed away from the sink, dropping the towel and pulling on my tank top and underwear. Maybe I should make peace and explain everything to Ryker. But it would be after the fact. *Would it even make a difference?*

I'd never given a shit before about what a man thought, and I damn sure hadn't cared about making peace. Now I was ready to track down my wolf and beg for forgiveness.

What has this man done to me?

I sighed heavily, stepping out of the bathroom. I skidded to a stop when I saw Ryker standing in my bedroom doorway, waiting.

"On the bed, and spread it wide," he growled.

I stilled. So this was how he wanted to play it. Now we were back on solid ground. Sex, I understood. No more of this emotional, touchy-feely bullshit. We'd fuck this out and move on.

I gave him a flirty smile. "Oh, I love where you're going with this." I winked at him. "Do you want to frisk me first, or should I assume the position?"

He coolly looked at me while shaking a bottle of oil. "Healing oil. Rosa said it should help with your cuts."

"You know you're nothing but a cock tease." I tried to hide my disappointment. "Okay, give it here and get the hell out." I reached for it.

He frowned. "Get on the bed."

I crawled onto the bed, stretching out facedown. I glanced back at him. "Like this?" I wiggled my ass and eyebrows at him.

"Light"—he impatiently slapped my ass—"spread your legs wide."

If he made me wait any longer, I was going to take matters into my own hands—I glanced at his cock—literally.

"Your wish is my command, alpha." I stretched my arms in front of me, gripping the sheets.

My heart raced as he knelt behind me.

His fingers dug into my hair, snatching my head back. "You should have thought about that shit when you deliberately failed to tell me about your father." He pulled away, easing toward the headboard, where he leaned against it and waited. "Come over here."

I sighed as I eased myself onto my knees. I crawled over to him and settled between his muscled legs with my back pressed against his chest. I bit my bottom lip when he dripped oil on my cuts, gently rubbing it in. God, this man had wonderful hands. I bit back a moan. I'd never wanted to fuck so badly before.

Focus, girl.

I cleared my throat. "Ryker, we need to talk."

"Yeah, we do."

A long moment passed before either of us spoke.

"I'm sorry." I sighed. "I should have told you about my father. Before today, I didn't even know he was alive." I paused. "Frankly, I didn't know a lot of things."

"And the Shadows?"

"I didn't know they even existed before today." I rolled my eyes as his hands slid along my thighs. "Believe me; finding out my grandfather is a lunatic is not exactly thrilling. And finding out he's trying to kidnap me . . . is damn frightening."

His hands stilled. "You should have told me."

"I couldn't. I swore to my mother I wouldn't."

He growled. "Don't blame this shit on her."

"Ryker—"

"You didn't tell me because you refused to let me in."

My body stiffened. "Let you in? You mean let you into my bed, right? From the first time you saw me, you viewed me as another conquest, so don't sit here and act any different."

"I'm honest enough with myself to say yes. But that changed. Everything changed. Nothing else will change for you or us if you can't even be honest with yourself."

I stayed silent. This was totally new territory for me, and I didn't know how to respond. "I'm not sure what you think is going to happen here, but this will never work."

"Tell me something. Why do you drink so much?"

My mouth dropped open. "What?"

He scoffed. "You heard me. Why do you drink so much?"

I hesitated a second too long. "Because it's fattening, and it's not good for me."

He laughed coldly. "So that's what you do? The first sign of a man caring for you, wanting you for more than a fuck toy, and you hide behind your mask?"

It stung a little that he'd figured me out. Hard and sweaty sex I could do, but relationships and commitment were a no-go.

"So you think you've got me figured out, huh?"

"Yes," he responded bluntly.

My calm façade broke. "Okay, I'm done." I scrambled off the bed and marched toward the door before stopping to think for a second.

I turned back to face him. He blankly stared at me.

"Look, I'm going to keep it real and blunt." I gestured wildly. "This thing between us has to fucking stop."

He arched a brow. "And what thing are you talking about?" He looked at me with smoldering eyes.

Shit. Shit. Shit. I felt my sex clench. I wanted this fucking arrogant motherfucker.

"Let's not play games. I suggest we bang this out—right here, right now. Get it out of our systems." I pulled my hair out of the ponytail, angrily shaking it out. "We do this, walk away, and get the hell on with business."

There—I'd said it. I was a big girl with no time for coy games.

He slowly stood up and widened his muscular legs. "As much as I love a good bang, you and I are not banging shit out. When I get you under me, it's going to be slow, hard, and memorable."

My heart stuttered. *Dammit!* "Okay, not my usual approach, but if it helps me get this itch out of my system, I'm all for it." I nervously licked my dry lips.

"Let's be clear, Light. There will be no out for you. I want you on a permanent basis." His lips tightened as he pointedly looked at me. "But I refuse to accept you like this."

His hand grabbed the back of my head. He kissed me, and I felt his canines against my tongue. But I didn't give a shit. I wanted him too badly. And I wanted him like this.

He pulled away.

My mouth dropped open with shock. "Ryker, I don't do permanent for a multitude of reasons. I'm not changing for any man."

"I'm not any man."

"Whatever." I scoffed.

On the inside, though, I agreed. He was not just any man. I took a shaky breath. The room was hot and uncomfortable.

"There's nothing wrong with alcohol in moderation. Drinking until you can't remember your name or until you black out is unacceptable. I need you sober."

"I am sober," I rasped.

His eyes narrowed. "Surprisingly. This is the first time I've seen you remotely coherent."

I gave him the middle finger. "Go fuck yourself, wolf-shifter."

"Now, is that nice?" He pulled me between his legs, gripping my hair.

I moaned in response, the edge of pain taking me right where I needed to be.

"We can have something great. You know that, right?"

I tried to pull away from him, but he held my head tight.

"I don't do sweet and romantic. I like it raw and rugged," I muttered between pants.

He looked like the type of man who would fuck me so hard and long that I would pass out from ecstasy right in the middle. Then he'd revive me, flip me over, and fuck me all over again. God, I wanted him. My mouth watered with need.

His sea-green wolf eyes glinted. "Do I look like a sweet and romantic kind of man?"

"No, it's . . ." I looked down to think. "It's . . . it's complicated."

"Light, there's nothing complicated about meeting a man you like and knowing what to do."

We both were silent.

Ryker leaned closer. I didn't move back; my eyes closed. He barely touched my lips with his.

I gulped, opening my eyes again. "What are you playing at, Ryker? I've seen the parade of women you've been through. I know the real alpha, the I-don't-give-a-shit you. So what's all this fluff?"

"This is the alpha who will change your world." He paused as his eyes softened. "I'm not trying to break you, Light. I love your wildness. In fact, I need it. But I need the real you"—he pressed a hand over my heart—"the one hiding in here, too afraid to show me the real you, not this shell of a woman."

My mouth hardened. "What you see is what you fucking get, Ryker. I'm wild and blunt, and I love alcohol and sex—lots of it." I cupped his crotch, feeling the hardness. *Damn, he's even big there.* I quickly let go. "And for some reason, you're not down to partake in that." I paused. "But I'm not afraid to go after what I want."

"All things I love about you. I'm not looking for a quick fuck with you. I'm looking for forever."

My eyes widened with shock. "Let's be clear. I'm broken, and I can't be fixed." I swallowed over the pain. "Every man I've been with couldn't deal with my mood swings, so they got what they wanted and left."

"I'm not every man. I'm your man, if you give us a chance."

"I can't." I decided the truth was needed. "I have real emotional issues that I'm dealing with. And I'm slipping into a dark rabbit hole that even I can't get out of." I blinked back the fear and emotions. "You need someone stable, a mate who can help you with the pack. I'm not her." I touched his cheek, feeling the tether tugging and pulsing between us. Sharply pulling back, I gritted my teeth. I couldn't put him through watching me slowly lose my mind. "I'm sorry, Ryker."

His face was like granite. "You can run, but you can't hide, Light. This is real. I can't force you to want to take a leap of faith." He gently pushed me away. "Come back to me when you're ready for a real man." He turned on his heels and exited.

I wrapped my arms around myself, and for the first time in my life, I let the salty tears of regret flow down my cheeks, unchecked.

❧ 14 ❧

LIGHTNING

I ROLLED OVER, pressing my face into my pillow when I heard the annoying ringing. It was too early, and I had just gotten to sleep after tossing and turning all night. Despite all my efforts, I couldn't get Ryker out of my head, which pissed me the hell off.

My cell stopped ringing. I sighed.

It started ringing again.

I grabbed it. "Yes?"

"Wake up, Sleeping Beauty," Reason drawled.

"What?" I paused. "And this had better not be about last night."

Reason laughed. "Not at all, princess of the Shadow lunatics. I knew one day you would be the leader of your own group of lunatics."

My lips curled up into a grin. "Thanks for poking me with a stick."

"I'm the daughter of a stone-cold killer. Believe me; I'm not judging." She paused. "By the way, Dad explained it all, and before you bitch about it, we're keeping the information within the circle."

"Make sure your coven does," I snapped.

Reason paused. "That's not what I called about. I have some information. When you left last night—"

I snorted. "Let's be clear. I didn't leave. I was dismissed."

"*O-kay*, after you were dismissed, I overheard Ryker telling my father—"

"Overheard?" I scoffed.

"You want to hear this shit or not?" she asked with an impatient tinge.

"Go on."

"Ryker said after his enforcers did some physically persuasive talking with Leo, he caved. Celina had paid him to break into the safe."

I lifted my sleep mask and sat up, more alert. "Celina? She paid him all that money?"

The escorts were independently wealthy, but that was a lot of money, even for her.

"No. She repeatedly fucked him for his safe-cracking services. He claims the Shadows paid him."

I gritted my teeth. "Ryker deliberately withheld important information. He should have told me this last night. I'm going to kick that wolf-shifter in the teeth."

"Isn't that what you did? Held back information?" She paused. "By the way, were you ever going to tell your best friend and lawyer about this warrior-Shadow-princess shit?"

"Of course."

"Mm-hmm," Reason muttered.

I was going to tell her . . . eventually. "Can we get back to Celina? Why would she want to steal our client list or, more importantly, help the Shadows?"

"You want to find out? I'm sure Celina's apartment can give us a hint as to why."

I pushed my tousled hair away from my face. "Give me an hour, then swing by and get me."

"And how are you going to escape from Ryker?"

I pursed my lips. "Let me worry about that."

Now I was pissed. Ryker was a damn hypocrite. All that bull-shit about trust, and he'd withheld the one piece of information I cared about—who had taken our list.

I slid off the bed, slipping into the bathroom to freshen up. After brushing my teeth and hair, I tugged my hair into a pony-tail with jerky movements. My mind raced as I prowled into the walk-in closet.

Why would Celina betray us? We'd had a good working relation-ship with her. Shit, she had been our top escort, and Credence O. had treated her as such. There was never even a sign that she was angry or resentful. *And what was the connection between her and the Shadows?* All of this was too strange and too much of a coin-cidence.

I pulled on a dangerously short, black-and-white knit mini dress, paired it with black knit leg warmers, and finished off the look with short, black suede booties. I stood by the door, strate-gizing on how to get away from Ryker undetected. *Fuck it.* I would wing it.

Ready to face my sexy Wolfie, I cracked open the door and padded across the penthouse, pausing only when my stomach rumbled embarrassingly loud.

Okay, eat first and then escape.

Within minutes, I quickly stepped into his gorgeous gourmet kitchen, practically salivating when I saw the espresso machine. Pushing the button, I watched excitedly as the rich, black coffee streamed into my cup. Greedily grabbing the cup, I moaned with pleasure as the mellow blend rolled over my tongue.

"This is so much better than sex."

"I beg to differ," Ryker drawled.

I jumped at his voice and quickly turned around, gawking at the large, black wolf tattoo covering the left side of his massive chest. Its fluffy tail swirled down, wrapping around his yummy, well-defined waist.

I caught myself and cleared my throat. "And since you refuse to make me a believer, forgive me if I don't take your word on that." I placed another cup under the machine to fill.

Leaning my hip against the granite kitchen counter, I boldly roamed my eyes up and down his body. The man was tan with bulging muscles. Hardened abs rippled downward to his low-slung lounge pants. He ran a hand through his sleep-tousled hair. *Damn, no man should look this fucking good in the morning.*

"By all means, check out the goods, darling." He grinned confidently, making no attempt to conceal the erection tenting the lightweight fabric of his pants.

I smiled over the rim of my cup. *This man is going to be the death of me.* I cleared my throat. *Get it together, Light. Focus. Reason is on her way.*

I drained my cup and set it down. "So let's talk breakfast. We'll have eggs, toast, and whatever else I can scrounge up." I turned to open the subzero refrigerator, hoping to distract myself from his delectable body.

RYKER

I INSTANTLY GOT HARD AGAIN at the sight of her curvy ass peeking out from underneath her dress, which looked as if it were meant to be a top. I wanted nothing more at this moment than to bend her over the counter and take her from behind, sliding deep into her. The desire was strong, but I restrained the temptation. I wouldn't give Light what she wanted—a quick fuck. No, I was determined to prove to her she was worth more to me.

I grabbed the espresso-filled cup, making sure to brush her arm. I smiled when she shivered deliciously.

"Did you like it?" I asked seductively.

She slammed the refrigerator closed and turned sharply, holding a carton of eggs and vegetables. "Did I like what, Wolfie?"

I locked eyes on hers, grabbing the eggs and vegetables and putting them on the countertop. She jammed her hands on her luscious hips.

She bit her bottom lip. "What?"

I stepped forward, caging her, making sure her body was flush against mine. "You examined me like a side of beef. And frankly, I fucking enjoyed it. Now all I want to know is did you like what you saw, darling?" I whispered in her ear.

❧ 16 ❧

LIGHTNING

I sucked in a breath as the hard bulge pressed against my stomach. Reaching between us, my hand gripped his cock, and he shut his eyes tight as a growl rumbled in his chest.

"I've made no secret about that, alpha." I gave him one more squeeze.

Our mouths were a breath away, the desire and tension almost more than I could take. Then I blinked, and his eyes snapped open. They were wild and sensual.

"I'm trying not to slam you onto this counter." He leaned into me, and just as quickly, he pulled back, his body shaking. "I don't want to take you like this, Light. I want you to understand that I want more . . . from you and us."

My pulse raced as his eyes turned wolf. I cupped his cheek, feeling the slide of his wolf underneath. My eyes widened. His beast was so close to the surface, fighting him for control. This was what Ryker fought every day to tame. He struggled like me. My struggle was my empath issues. His was controlling his beast. And he didn't want to fail like every male in his family did.

"How bad?" I whispered.

He shrugged his muscled shoulders. "Some days, it's bearable."

Something stirred within me. I desperately wanted to end his pain. Grabbing his face, my fingers tingled strangely. His beast pressed forward.

"No!" He took a breath. "I wouldn't do that right now."

"Quiet, alpha," I answered. Going on pure instinct, I glided my fingers across his jaw. A soft pulse of energy whipped through my body, and the beast fell back.

Ryker's eyes transformed back to human. He leaned his head against mine, letting out a sigh of relief. "What did you do?"

I shrugged. "I don't know." That was the truth, and it was what made my empath abilities so damn scary. It was unpredictable.

"Are you ready to tell me what you are?"

"Maybe . . . someday, if this thing works out between us." Honestly, that was an outcome I highly doubted.

"Maybe?" Ryker demanded.

I nearly swallowed my tongue when he lifted me, setting me on the countertop. The cold granite felt delicious against my ass. I smiled, thinking about the ass prints that would be left. He gently pushed me back, one hand firmly grabbing ahold of my wrists while his legs forced my knees apart. His free hand ripped my panties off and slid into my pussy, two fingers pushing inside, stretching me open. I moaned as I clenched those fingers tight.

❧ 17 ❧

RYKER

LIGHT MOANED, and my cock hardened even more at the sound.

Yeah, Light was a complicated woman, but I wanted her —forever.

My fingers stilled as I straightened, "Are you ready to give me what I need? What we both need?"

Frowning, she asked, "What?"

"I want your submission. I want your body, heart, and soul." I stilled her hips. Otherwise, her constant grinding would have me coming all over her. "I want your beautiful body under me, over me, whatever way I can think of, for the rest of our lives."

She looked away, an expression of intense thought on her face. I hid his surprise when I realized I'd actually gotten her to consider it. I knew what I wanted. And maybe, from the moment I'd met her, my beast had known.

She tried to move away from me, but I held her tight.

And I waited.

Finally, she looked at me, her eyes clear but worried. "There's so much you don't know about me. Shit, there's so much I don't know about you."

"We're Others, Light. We don't play games like humans. You

and I know the difference between straight-up physical attraction and something more. This, between us, is something more."

I arched into her body as I sucked her tongue into my mouth. I couldn't hold it back anymore, not with her soft and pliant in my arms. Her tongue slid around the tip of mine and then rubbed under it. I let my hands slide up to her neck and then down her body to her hips. I leaned in and kissed her throat before biting the spot.

I traced a finger over the small tattoo of a lightning bolt on her left hip. "Submit, Light."

"Not on your life, alpha."

Rubbing my nose against her neck, I growled, "Is that your final answer?"

"Yes."

I sighed. She still wasn't ready. I offered my hand, pulling her off the countertop. I kissed her hard on the lips and stepped back.

"Enjoy your breakfast, darling. I need a cold shower to get rid of this hard-on." I turned on my heel and exited the kitchen.

As far as I was concerned, this wasn't the end. It was just the beginning.

❦ 18 ❦

LIGHTNING

Reason looked over to me.

I'd felt her heavy stare since I got into the SUV, but I didn't care. I was still confused about my kitchen tryst with Ryker. We had been on the cusp of something great. Then I'd blinked, and he had left, walking away without another word. He'd left me standing alone in the kitchen, and for what seemed like hours, I'd fought the urge to go running after him like an idiot.

I frowned, staring at the passing Manhattan scenery. *Does he actually want me as his mate?* I bit my lower lip. *He actually wants me to be the alpha female of his pack. Is he insane?*

"I've never seen you this quiet, Light." Reason smirked. "So have you fucked him yet?"

My jaw dropped. "What? No!"

Reason laughed. "The guy is crazy about you. And despite your little act, you're crazy about him."

I glared at her.

"Oh, what? Was that supposed to be some big secret?" Reason smiled quickly. "So if you didn't fuck him, what's really going on between you and Ryker?"

I tried to give Reason an innocent look but failed. "Something happened. Something changed. It's been weird between us lately."

"Lately?" She paused. "Light, it's been weird since your whole X-rated foreplay scene in my office."

I stared at her, confused. "No, this is different. He's different. After he gave me his ultimatum . . ." I gulped. "He wants me as his mate. That's crazy."

"And you said no."

I angrily looked at her. "Of course I did. Look at me. I'm a fucking unstable mess. And now that I know I'm the evil spawn of the Shadows, shit is bound to go downhill fast."

"But your empath symptoms are not as bad since you met Ryker. I can tell."

I froze. *How in the hell did she know that?* "That's not the point. I can't give him what he wants." I incredulously looked at her. "Can you picture me as his mate? It's just not me."

"You can't or you won't? There's a big fucking difference."

"Don't psychoanalyze me, hybrid," I hissed. "The whole point I'm trying to make is when I said no, he pulled away." My teeth clenched. "He had his fingers in my vagina, and he walked away like nothing had happened." I arched a brow. "Who the hell does that shit?"

Reason snickered. "God, that was genius."

I jabbed her in the side.

Reason grinned. "What? It was." She paused. "Put it this way; can you blame him? He offered you his heart, and you said, *No, thank you. I'll take your cock instead.*" She laughed. "Now, who does that shit?" she scoffed. "Lightning Credence—that's who."

I was unnerved by the observation but tried to play it off. "I've seen what offering your heart can do—tear you apart when it's abused."

Reason banged on the steering wheel. "Oh my fucking God! You got your heart broken years ago. Get the fuck over it. Everyone knew Nolan was a fucking prick. But you know what pisses me the fuck off the most? You're such a damn hypocrite.

You're so ready to give me and Storm relationship advice, but you can't take it from either of us."

She pointed at me. "I don't give a shit if you don't talk to me ever again for saying this, but it has to be said. When you get back to Ryker's penthouse, you put on your best sexy dress with a pair of fuck-me-please heels. Then I want you to prance around like the sex kitten you are and tell him you're willing to give it a chance."

I stared at Reason. I had never seen her so mad. She was right, but I'd be damned if I'd admit it right now. I was never going to be perfect. Ryker knew this and fucking accepted it.

"Anything else?" I asked dryly.

"I wasn't done, empath," she said, pursing her lips. "Then get on your damn knees and submit. And don't forget to deep-throat his damn big cock like the champion I know you are. That's all. I'm done with this conversation."

I was still silent but allowed myself a small smile at Reason's statement. Reason gave me a piercing gaze. I bit my lip but didn't respond to her rant.

"Yeah, but, Reason—"

"I know. You're dealing with stuff. But you cannot ask him to wait forever."

I didn't respond.

Reason continued. "Unless, of course, you're okay with him pulling away."

"What if it doesn't work?"

"It will."

I thought for a second, quiet as I considered Reason's advice.

Reason pulled her SUV up to Celina's apartment building and watched as I got out of the car, giving me one last pointed look. "Don't think you were saved by the bell, Lightning Credence. As your friend, I'm not going to let this drop. When we get done with this, we're going to have a long talk."

"I thought we just did," I mumbled under my breath.

We walked up to the door, stepping into the palatial lobby.

The human concierge smiled at us. I felt his lust slithering all over me.

Reason glided up to him, trailing her fingers over his wrist. "Hello, Frank."

He smiled. "Apartment number twenty-three." He discreetly slid a set of keys across the counter. "When can I see you again?" he asked with desperation written all over his face.

She ran her fingers over his hand before accepting the keys. "I'll call you." She winked at him before pushing me toward the elevator.

I waited until the door slid closed and asked, "What was that?"

She smiled prettily, displaying her canines. "The power of vampire persuasion."

I arched a brow as we slipped out of the elevator, walking over to Celina's door.

"I met him last night at the kink party. He had an itch; I scratched it."

She inserted the key in the door and opened it. We entered cautiously, looking around. The place was a mess. The leather couch was slashed. I stepped over broken glass.

"Whoa. What's going on here?" I whispered. Something caught my eye. I stopped. There was a bloodstain on the floor that looked wet. "Look, fresh blood."

Reason walked over and stared. "Exactly what type of shit was Celina into?"

I pulled out my cell and turned slowly, taking photos of every angle of the room, clicking, clicking, and clicking on the patch of blood on the living room floor. "How the hell would I know? Someone kills her, and then her place gets trashed? Not a coincidence."

Reason stared at the mess. "They were searching for something specific. You don't rip through a couch unless you've run out of places to look. Maybe they didn't find what they were hunting for."

I surveyed the apartment. "Maybe it's still here, but it's too well hidden. Did you confirm how she died?"

"Her body was found in her car . . . burned beyond recognition. Extra crispy."

"Ew." I scrolled through my phone, dialing Celina's number. "C'mon. C'mon, answer."

There was a phone ringing behind me. It sounded like it was coming from the couch. I searched the cushions and started to take the couch apart. There was blood under the cushions. The ringing got louder, and I found the cell. It was Celina's phone with lots of missed calls. My heart stopped. One of the missed calls was from Ryker.

Why was Ryker calling Celina?

I scrolled through her call history. She'd made lots of calls. I recognized many of our client names and numbers, and then I saw Ryker's number again.

Was he fucking her? And most importantly, why didn't he say he knew Celina?

"What's with the look on your face?" Reason stared at me. "What's on the phone?"

"Lots of calls from and to our clients," I said.

Reason shrugged. "So Celina fucked around a lot."

My fingers clenched. "She made several calls to Ryker."

"So?" Her mouth dropped open. "Oh . . . you think they were sleeping together?"

I slipped the cell into my bag. "Don't know. Don't care."

"Uh-huh."

I glared at her. "What's that supposed to mean?"

Reason stepped back with a smile. "Nothing."

I walked away, heading toward the back of the apartment. "Not once did he mention he knew Celina. Don't you think that's strange?"

Reason strolled behind me. "Celina knew a lot of powerful men. She wasn't your top wolf-shifter escort for nothing."

I stepped into Celina's bedroom, looking around with wild

eyes. "Shit. I can't believe I'm jealous of a fucking dead woman." I banged my hand on the dressing table. "She fucked him. She actually fucked him."

"You don't know that."

My eyes narrowed. "Celina was a straight-up sex fiend. It's what made her the most requested escort."

"Ryker's not a Boy Scout, but he would have told you if he'd fucked her."

I scowled. "I don't want to talk about this anymore. Let's finish searching this damn apartment and get the hell out of here."

"Fine." Reason walked into the closet.

I searched through Celina's drawers and found nothing. "Did you find anything?"

Reason stepped out of the closet. "No. But I didn't think anyone could have more stilettos than you."

The apartment door slammed open.

"Someone's coming," I hissed.

"Shit." Reason picked up a pair of stilettos, handing them to me.

"What the hell am I supposed to do with these?" I whispered.

"The damn heel—use it to stab whoever's outside," Reason whispered back while pulling out a Taser from her bag.

Wood creaked. I put a finger to my lips. Someone was coming. The footsteps got closer. We both froze, undecided on hiding or standing our ground. We didn't have time to choose. Jackal and Rip stormed into the bedroom with guns drawn.

"Dammit! You two scared the shit out of us," I snapped. "How did you find me?"

They both holstered their guns.

Jackal winked at me. "We put a tracker on your cell, sweetness."

My eyes narrowed. "Ryker ordered it?"

"Of course, and you should prepare to bat those pretty little eyes when you go downstairs. He's pissed," Rip responded.

"We'll see about that." I stomped past him, exiting the apartment.

I was silent as we rode the elevator down.

Jackal stared at Reason. "I can't believe you broke into an apartment, lawyer."

Reason rolled her eyes. "It was necessary."

"It was criminal trespassing," he snapped.

She coldly studied him. "*To-may-to, to-mah-to.*" She paused. "And the next time you sneak up behind me, I'll show you how my Taser works, shifter."

Jackal stepped closer. "Promise?"

I pursed my lips. "Will you two get a damn room?" I stepped out of the elevator, leaving them behind.

I smiled when Reason caught up with me. "Still working the Jackal situation?"

"Yep." She smiled. "He's not ready to admit he has a hard-on for a sexy vampire. But I'm working on it." She winked.

I laughed. "God, I love you."

She pulled me into a hug. "So remember, no panties when you put on your sexy dress."

I frowned.

"You can do this." Reason finished.

I sighed heavily. "Okay, okay. I just . . . I-I have to find the right time."

She pursed her lips. "Yeah, you do that."

We walked outside the building to see an angry Ryker leaning against his SUV. I turned to glance at Reason.

"On second thought, maybe you should wait a bit." Reason angled toward her SUV. "I . . . gotta go." She hightailed it away, leaving me to watch Ryker.

"This is going to be fun." I groaned, walking past Rip and Jackal with my head held high.

Ryker held the door open without a word. I slid in, scooting to the farthest end of the backseat. Ryker got in and slammed the door. I impatiently drummed my fingers. He neutrally looked at me but didn't utter a word. He didn't have to. I could feel his anger seeping out of his pores. His rage was mixed with frustration.

Wait . . . emotions?

I'd never felt anyone's emotions but humans. This thing . . . this connection between us was redefining everything about me and my powers.

I looked out the window, trying to sort out this mess, but the silence dragged on way too long, and it was killing me.

"Nothing to say?" I asked.

He silently stared at me.

I uncomfortably looked at him.

"That was irresponsible and reckless," he stated calmly. Yet his emotions were translating something completely different—anger and disappointment. Then a wall went up, and I felt absolutely nothing. He'd intentionally shut me out.

Hurt, I verbally attacked. "Why didn't you tell me Celina hired Leo to break into our safe? Or about the connection with the Shadows?"

"I told Lia and Ava. That was enough," he commented curtly.

"But you didn't tell me. Why?"

"Because I knew you would do some impulsive, foolish shit to get yourself in trouble." He glared at me. "You have Shadows actively hunting you, and you're traipsing around Manhattan like it doesn't mean shit."

My lips tightened. "I can handle myself."

He scoffed. "That's not the damn point." He glared. "The point is you knew what could happen if the Shadows got their hands on you. And it didn't occur to you to come to me and ask for help." His mouth tightened. "Or worse, it did occur to you, and you chose not to. Now what does that say about us? Not much, if you ask me."

"I'm not stupid. And I can defend myself." I paused. "You

know what? I'm tired of this shit. You tell me you want something real with me. In essence, you want me to trust you. But guess what? Getting my trust starts with telling me the truth."

"I've always told you the truth."

I jabbed him in the chest with a finger. "Really? So did you fuck her?"

His eyes narrowed. "Can you be more specific? There've been a lot of *hers*."

I was appalled and confused at his behavior and cool tone. I wanted to smack the arrogance off his face. "Celina Rouse," I gritted out.

"Don't know her," he responded matter-of-factly.

I saw red. He was a liar. All men were fucking liars. Flashes of every time Nolan had lied about the numbers on his cell zipped through my head.

I dug into my bag and threw Celina's cell at Ryker's head. He caught it midair.

"Your number is on her cell. Remember now?" I sneered.

Rip pulled into the underground garage. He and Jackal sat there waiting. Ryker calmly placed the cell on the seat between us.

"I'll see you two upstairs," Ryker snapped, waiting as they exited. "First, I'm not a liar. And I damn sure would never lie to you. Second, I didn't know Celina."

I arched a brow. I was trying to tread carefully, but it wasn't working.

"Let me finish before you start spinning a fucked-up story in your head." He paused. "When I became alpha, she called me, offering her services to me as some kind of freebie fuck. I declined. But that didn't stop her from calling. She'd even show up, uninvited, at events I attended. But nothing happened. She was way too pushy and not my type."

My eyes narrowed. "Why would she call you? Our escorts have an exclusive contract with us. And they work the clients we present."

"That's what I thought, but she said she freelanced from time to time."

My mind reeled. *Did Celina steal our client list to set up shop for herself?* "How did she get your number?"

"She said she got it from a business colleague."

"The first time you executed your contract, you specifically requested Celina for Knox."

He frowned. "When I was thinking about getting an escort for Knox as a birthday gift, she came highly recommended by Noah. I didn't care. I wanted Knox's introduction to sex with a female shifter to be memorable. That's it."

"The same Noah you saw on the video footage, having a secret meeting?" I didn't have a good feeling about this. "This still doesn't explain why there's an incoming call from you." I handed him her cell.

"What?" he scowled before scrolling through her incoming calls. "I never called her."

"That's your number."

"So now I'm like every man who fucked you over? You want to shove me away?"

I was momentarily speechless. My heart was racing as I fought the fear and the tears. He knew too much; his words cut too deep.

"Don't make this about us," I said.

He glared. "I'm sorry; tell me how this isn't about us?" he growled, opening the door. "I can't be here right now." He exited the car.

I sighed, refusing to try to stop him. Sliding out, I leaned against the car, waiting for him to walk away . . . again.

His face tightened, as if he knew exactly what I was thinking. "I never called her. I never fucked her. You either believe me or you don't."

"Why are you telling me this?"

"I think you should know what kind of person you're dealing with."

One part of me wanted him to fight . . . for me, for us. The other part of me was afraid he actually would.

"This conversation is over." I turned on my heel, walking away.

"Light, stop." He grabbed my arm.

I swung around. "First, don't touch me." I raised a trembling finger. My emotions were raw, scattered. I honestly didn't know what I wanted anymore. And like a coward, I was too afraid to figure it out. "Second, don't touch me."

"They will try to kidnap you again. And if you don't care about that, at least think about how that's going to effect the people who love you. Do you really want to put your mother and aunt through that? And what about Storm?"

"And what about you, Ryker?"

He shrugged his wide shoulders. "I don't want anything to happen to you. I'm your protector and your friend," he grunted.

It was definitely not what I had expected. My jaw dropped. "Is that what we are? Friends?"

Friends? That was like the kiss of fucking death. He might as well have said he was no longer interested in being with someone like me.

"I don't know what we are. We kiss, and then we never talk about it. I stick my fingers in your pussy, but we never talk about it. We almost fuck, but we never talk about it. So I've got no clue what we are." His jaw tightened. "But I know I don't want to see you walk away from me!"

I shoved him. "Yeah, well, watch me."

I stormed past him, but he wasn't done.

"This is about you needing a place to hide."

It took me a second to respond. His words hurt more than I'd thought they would.

I stopped, turning back to him. "You don't know me, Ryker. You think you do, but you don't."

"I know enough to know you hide in these nowhere relationships with men you don't love. You could be happy, Light. You deserve to be happy. But you're afraid."

I didn't move. "You know what we are, Ryker? We are over. Now leave me the fuck alone."

He coldly stared at me. "Your wish is my command, Light."

❧ 19 ❧

LIGHTNING

AN HOUR LATER, I was sitting in the serene environment of the private meditation terrace overlooking lower Manhattan. I sighed, dialing the one person I wanted to talk to right now.

"Storm?"

"Is everything all right? Light? Talk to me." Storm's voice was husky from sleep.

"Is Knox there?"

"Yeah, but he's sleeping. Finally. Jesus, the man is a sex machine. I feel like I rode a horse."

I laughed. "Well, you know what they say; ride a wolf-shifter, save a horse."

Storm muffled her snicker. "Stop, you're going to make me wake him up."

Knox grumbled in the background. "I'm not sleeping. I'm giving you time to recoup for round three."

Storm groaned. "Go to sleep, Knox."

"Sounds like you have it hard . . . literally," I pointed out playfully.

I heard scuffling and a door slam.

"Light? Sorry. I had to escape the room. Plus, I can hear in your voice that you really want to talk." She paused. "What's going on? Issues with Ryker?"

"No. No issues." I curled my legs under me, enjoying the rooftop deck space with its brilliant three-hundred-sixty-degree views of Manhattan. "Nothing a couple shots of Patrón can't resolve."

"Uh-huh."

I groaned. "Okay, the man is making me crazy."

"Ryker?"

"Yes, Storm, Ryker. What the hell? Keep the fuck up."

"Uh-huh."

"What does that mean?"

"Reason told me everything. And I know you like him—a lot."

I sputtered, "I don't like him. He's an arrogant asshole with a stick lodged sideways up his ass."

"So tell me what's really going on."

I wiped my now damp forehead. Dammit, I needed to keep it together. And even though I hadn't seen him since our argument, I could still sense him somewhere at the other end of the penthouse. I pressed my fingers along my temple, trying to ease the pressure from the stress. It didn't work. There was one person who could do that now, and he was not my ideal choice for the job.

"Just stressed," I responded flatly, curling up into the plush cushions.

"Uh-huh. I can tell you're hiding something. First, start explaining why our mental connection isn't helping relieve your pain."

I exhaled noisily, hesitating to give voice to my worst fears. "You've been replaced."

Storm was quiet.

"Did you hear me? When I was around Detective Prick, it was eerily silent when Ryker touched me. I felt nothing. No irritating human emotions. Just"—I swallowed hard—"calm."

Storm cleared her throat. "Oh my God! Ryker is your mate?" she hissed. "Demi was right about the prophecy? She's never right."

I rolled my eyes. "Surprise, she got this right."

"So what's the problem? Zone in on the shifter and make him yours."

"It's not going to work."

"Bullshit. You're upset."

"No." I paused. "Yes, I am. I fucked up, and now it seems like he's pulling away."

"Have you asked him why?"

"I know why. I pushed him away."

"You're afraid he'll reject you because you're an empath," Storm stated.

"No!" I blurted out too forcefully. "No. What? Why would you even say that?" I continued. "That's not even the point."

"Then tell me. What's the point, Light? Because I don't understand a damn thing you're saying right now. He balances you and wants you, but you're pushing him away."

I hated how she always had a way of cutting to the chase. "Wait, what? What—what do you mean?"

"When he asked you to give the relationship a chance, what did you say?"

"I wasn't ready to hear it then."

"What do you think he's telling you with his behavior?" Stormed probed.

I stopped to think. "That . . . maybe . . . he's changed his mind?" I slumped in the chair. "What if I waited too long?"

"You weren't waiting, Light. You were making sure you could give him what he needed . . . all of you."

"Yeah, but in the meantime, he's moved on."

"Or he's protecting himself by not taking any more emotional risks."

I bit my lower lip. It was time for the truth. "He scares the shit out of me. He's the one man who has changed everything I thought I knew about myself." *He's the one man who's stripped away my mask and laid me out, bare and vulnerable.* "I've spent my whole life building a fortress and defending myself from being hurt again."

"Listen to me; tell Ryker you're an empath."

"No."

"I can't force you, but I'm done with secrets and walking on eggshells. Look at what it almost got me. If I had been upfront with Knox about the Credence Curse, I would have avoided that whole nasty incident with Luke. And maybe he wouldn't be running loose right now. So you think about that."

I was silent.

Storm continued. "Tell him. Believe me; I know it's scary to put your heart out there, but he's worth it."

"Yeah, until he knows I'm sick. Wolf-shifters run away from the weak or take advantage of it."

My lips pursed, remembering what Nolan had done to me. I hadn't known where he began and I ended. It had been sick and twisted, and the thought filled me with rage and queasiness.

"If you're still harping on Nolan, let that shit go. Besides, I'm not entirely convinced dark magic wasn't at work when you were with him."

"I can't let it go. And I can't trust any man to do the right thing," I verbalized

I hated feeling this way, but a whole lot of shitty life lessons had taught me that nothing good comes out of trusting men. They were good for one thing—instant gratification. I'd leave the sappy love-relationship shit to weak-minded women.

"Do you know he refuses to sleep with me?"

Storm snickered. "And how is that bad?"

"Shifters are innately sexual beings. And with my sucky luck, I've found the one shifter in New York who refuses to fuck me. No, he's waiting until I give myself to him—mind, body, and soul. Who the hell says shit like that anymore?"

Storm exhaled tiredly. "Show him who you really are, Light.

Let him in. He's a good man, and he wants you—the real you. Any man who refuses to fuck you until he gets the whole package is worth the risk. Isn't that what you told me about Knox? You're a hypocrite," Storm snapped. "You can give out advice about taking chances, but you can't accept it. Now pull on your big-girl panties and show him what he's getting—the real you, not the party girl Light. Show him the pain you deal with every day. Let him behind the curtains. If he runs, which I highly doubt he will, then he wasn't for you. But if he stays . . . he's a fucking keeper."

I dashed away the tears rolling down my cheeks. That was exactly what I was afraid of—that he would stay, and one day, he would regret it when the going got rough.

My body stiffened when I felt his presence before he even said a word. I looked over my shoulder to find him standing there, looking gorgeous but deadly.

"Pack meeting. There's new information you should hear," he declared before turning on his heel and walking away.

Pack meeting?

My pulse raced at the thought of belonging to him and being a part of his pack.

"Hey, Storm. Let me call you back."

"Okay. Think about what I said."

"I will." I hung up the phone and walked into the penthouse.

No one was in the living room, so I walked farther in, moving toward the voices. I hesitated for a second before stepping into the office.

Ryker looked over at me. "We need your help with something."

He nodded over to the two interactive whiteboards. One was blank; the other was a murder board with information on everyone who had been killed so far. Soar circled some names and then stepped back, staring at the board.

I appraised Ryker. "Any news on the hunt for our client list?"

Ryker crossed his arms. "No. But the good news is no more clients have shown up dead."

"Yet." Jackal finished.

I walked up to Soar and stared at the board. I used my finger, wrote *Shadows*, and then drew a line from it, connecting it to Celina's name. "There's a pattern. And we're missing it." I wrote Greco's name and circled it.

The entire team looked skeptical.

"Why are we doing this again?" Bones demanded with a pained look on his face.

Ignoring him, I looked over at Ryker. "Did you find the name of the person who owns Swodah Unified?" I inquired.

"His name is Baptiste Thomas," Ryker responded.

"So what else do we know so far?" I questioned.

"The Shadows paid Greco to break into your safe. And Celina slept with him as some sort of added bonus," he commented.

My face tightened. "So she stole the list for them?"

"Exactly," Soar interjected, "and now that she's dead, we don't know if she gave them the list or hid it."

I frowned. "I think she hid it. Someone broke into her apartment and tore it apart, looking for something. It's safe to say they were looking for the list."

Bones snorted and then paced back and forth. "That shit doesn't make any sense. Why would she steal the list for them?"

Jackal stared at him. "You all right, man?"

Bones bristled. "Yes! But we're standing here making up shit as we go."

Ryker and Jackal exchanged a brief look. Something was going on, but I couldn't delve into that right now. Something about Celina was nagging me.

I tapped Soar. "Anything else we're missing?"

He shrugged. "We already know the Shadows figured out how to harvest Others' organs."

Turning to stare at the whiteboard, I tiredly blew out,

"Okay." I continued. "Well, we also know the Shadows are buying a shitload of Manhattan property. But why?" I tapped my chin before drawing a money sign on the board. "You and I know Manhattan property is not cheap, so they're spending more money than they're bringing in from the sale of organs." I turned to stare at them. "They need more organs."

"That means they need to go big. Get more organs, fast," Rip theorized.

"But they only want the strongest Others. That's why they've been going after Others who are enforcers and seconds-in-command," Ryker interjected.

"They would need to find a meeting or maybe an event, something big with plenty of alphas or seconds-in-command," Soar observed.

"Yeah, but if that were the case, why didn't they stage an attack at Vivica's party?" Bones demanded.

Ryker laughed. "Not all the alphas are into kink—not in public, at least. Besides, Vivica's clients aren't only Others. They're humans, too."

I looked at the whiteboard. "Wait a second. Your gala tonight. No humans are invited."

Soar scowled. "Shit! She's right. We'll have to beef up security."

"If I were the Shadows, that's where I'd hit." I determinedly looked at Ryker. "So it's settled. I'll be ready at eight. That's not a problem, is it?"

Ryker frowned. "It might be dangerous."

I walked over to him and gently kissed him before stepping back. "I'm ready to trust my alpha, as you should be ready to trust me." I smiled. "If the Shadows want to bring it, then we'll be there to stop them . . . together." I turned on my heel, leaving Ryker stunned.

☙ 20 ❧

LIGHTNING

I STOOD IN MY CLOSET, wrapped in a towel, frantically looking over dresses. "Not this one." I pushed it out of the way. I looked at another, a couture red dress that was nearly see-through. "God, what was I thinking when I bought this?"

There was a knock at the door.

"Who is it?" I peeked out to see Rosa sauntering in, looking spectacular.

Her golden-tan skin contrasted beautifully with her skintight black evening gown. It was unfair how beautiful she was.

I smiled saucily. "Look who's filling out her dress like a stripper."

Rosa twirled around. "And if I play my cards right tonight, I might get some dollar bills stuck down my dress by a sexy wolf-shifter."

I growled playfully. "Go get him."

She winked. "I plan on it."

I stared at the box she was clutching. "What's that?"

Rosa smiled, extending the huge box. "Special delivery from Ryker."

I warily gazed at the box. "Is it a rattlesnake? Poisonous gas?"

She curiously examined me.

I sheepishly looked at her. "In case he didn't tell you, we had a horrible argument, and I said some not-so-nice things, things I'm not fucking proud of right about now."

"No, it's not a snake or gas. He would never hurt you, Light. He likes you too much."

I rolled my eyes, grabbing the box. "Yeah, likes me," I grumbled while opening the box and pulling the tissue wrap aside. "Oh." I pulled out a stunning backless gray gown. "Well . . ." I cleared my throat. "Okay, he likes me a little."

Rosa sat at the edge of the bed and smiled proudly. "That dress tells me he likes you more than a little." Her smile disappeared. "So why are you pretending like you don't want him?"

I fidgeted. "It's complicated."

She looked at me with clear green eyes that seemed to reach into my soul, reading everything. "It's an ex-boyfriend."

My eyes widened because she'd gotten it that fast. "Yes."

"A good-looking ex who was hung like a horse?"

I couldn't help my smile. "He wasn't that good-looking, but, Jesus . . . he was hung."

"And?"

I dropped the dress on the bed. "I was just out of college and wasn't into relationships due to all the Credence Curse omen shit. So I played around and made a lot of bad mistakes with men. And one day, all of my bad decisions caught up with me when I met Nolan, a wolf-shifter." I stared into space. "I knew it from the first moment I met him." I smiled sadly. "I should have run away as fast as I could, but I didn't."

"He cheated on you," Rosa guessed.

I laughed coldly. "No. If it were that simple, I would have gotten over the experience years ago." I swallowed, tasting the bitterness in my mouth, thinking about how bad things had gotten. "I lost a piece of myself to him. I can't describe how, even now. He started controlling my interactions with my family, the clothes I wore, where I hung out or didn't. The sad part is I should have known. I ignored my instincts. I gave away power.

And ultimately, I turned my back on my family because they hated him—and rightly so. My whole world started revolving around him, and he loved it." I pointedly looked at her. "It was freaky because it wasn't the type of woman I was. The thing is I knew the relationship was toxic, but the more I tried to pull away, the more I got sucked into his web of manipulation."

She worriedly looked at me. "That sounds more like dark magic."

I stared at her. "See? That's exactly what Storm said." I shrugged. "I don't know what to believe. All I know is things got so bad that I started losing track of time. Days ran into weeks. I stopped thinking. I was like some fucking zombie. When my family staged an intervention, I knew I had to leave him, but he begged me to stay. He even planned a romantic weekend trip to California."

Rosa's mouth dropped open. "He was trying to hide you from your family."

"How did you know that?"

Rosa was freaking me out.

"He was a manipulative asshole," Rosa noted simply. "What happened?"

"Put it like this; I woke up to the sound of the door being broken down. It was Storm rescuing me." I licked my lips. "Apparently, I had been missing for weeks. And Nolan was nowhere to be found." I gritted my teeth. "The bastard had me holed up in some luxury beachside villa." I clenched my fists, just thinking about it. "After Storm hauled me home, I couldn't even remember my fucking name for days. My mom had me examined for drugs, but—get this—I wasn't drugged. My fucking system was clean."

Rosa pursed her lips. "Dark magic."

I arched a brow. "Why does everyone keep saying that? It wasn't dark magic. I was weak. I let him manipulate me, take my life away, take my family away. I have to own up to the woman he made me."

Rosa wrapped an arm around me. "You are way too hard on yourself. The bastard knew how strong you were and manipulated you with magic. All the signs are there, honey." She grabbed my face. "You're mad at yourself for something you couldn't control."

My hands trembled. "I promised myself I would never let that happen again."

Rosa scowled. "If you're comparing my nephew to him, then I fucking take offense."

I gave her a small smile. "I know Ryker is nothing like him."

She looked at me, confused. "Okay, if that's the case, then what's stopping you from giving him a chance to prove it?"

"Now? Nothing. I decided hours ago that I want the crazy alpha. Now he's the one who's angry with me."

Rosa clucked her tongue. "So that's why he left with Soar."

My back straightened. "What the hell? He's not going to the gala tonight?"

"Oh, he's going. He said he had a meeting to go to first." Her face tightened. "He left instructions for Jackal and Rip to escort you to the gala."

"Oh, hell no! That asshole ditched me?" I jabbed a finger at her. "I told you he was pissed."

She crossed her arms. "So? Are you going to fix the problem?"

"Oh, I'm going to fix it all right." I stood. "He said he wanted me—mind, body, and soul. And I'll be damned if I let him renege on a motherfucking offer." My eyes narrowed. "The gloves are off. And I plan on fighting dirty to get him back."

Rosa clapped her hands with glee. "That's what I'm talking about. So how are you going to chase him down?"

"I never chase a man, but since I want Ryker so fucking much"—I winked at her—"I might power-walk."

Rosa pumped her fist in the air. "I love you Credence women." She stood and walked toward the door. "Get dressed. I'll see you at the gala. I have a surprise for you and the birthday boy." She exited with an extra pep in her step.

I dropped the towel and pulled on the gown. I fluffed my hair while walking into the closet and examined myself in the floor-to-ceiling mirror. The gown's plunging back revealed my none-too-discreet tattoo of a witch riding a broom on my shoulder blade and a large tattoo of roses, which sprawled from my lower back to the left side of my waist. I put on my vintage silver cuff bracelet designed with an intricate wolf and a connecting wolf ring, and I smiled.

Now I was ready.

Tonight, I planned on making Ryker mine. I wanted him, and I was willing to put my heart on the line to get him.

Watch out, Wolfie. Your alpha female is coming to get you.

~

I STEPPED OUT OF THE ELEVATOR, STRIDING LIKE A supermodel working the runway. I smiled when I saw Jackal and Rip standing impatiently by the limo. Their jaws dropped.

"Nice dress," Jackal commented.

Rip smirked. "Yeah, what there is of it."

I saucily winked at them. "Well, you can thank your alpha." I examined their custom-made tuxedos. "Wow! You two clean up nicely," I teased before sliding into the back of the limo.

They laughed before getting in. Jackal and Rip quickly looked at me as the limo pulled out of the garage and sped through Manhattan.

"Ryker had a meeting, but he'll meet us at the gala," Jackal commented.

I pursed my lips and rolled my eyes. "You mean he's mad at me," I responded sarcastically. "I know. I'll straighten out the alpha when I get there. No one stands me up."

Rip shook his head. "Oh shit, our alpha is in trouble."

I crossed my legs. "You got that right," I drawled as we pulled up to the hotel.

The driver opened the door.

"Come on, shifters, we have a party to start," I said.

We headed past the paparazzi and into the hotel. Men in tuxedoes escorted their diamond-encrusted ladies through the huge front doors. White-gloved security staffers politely scanned guests with handheld metal detectors. I smiled at the envious stares of females as Jackal and Rip flanked me while we waded through the high-society Others' world.

As we advanced into the ballroom, the live band playing a popular rock song punctuated the crescendo of conversation. We glided into the sea of guests who were drinking, dancing, and conversing. The party was in full swing.

"We're going to mill around. We want to make sure security has everything covered," Jackal whispered in my ear.

"I'm not worried. Go."

I watched them both walk off before I approached the circular bar. The bartender abandoned making a drink to come over to me.

"Lemon martini," I ordered before leaning against the bar, doing what I loved to do—watch Others.

My eyes narrowed. It was the same crowd, different event. The only thing I was grateful for was the event was attended only by Others, so I wouldn't have to deal with annoying human emotions driving me crazy.

The band abruptly stopped playing. Guests looked to the stage.

Rosa stepped onto the riser, looking stunning. She took the microphone and played up to the crowd before giving them a beauty-contestant smile. "Thank you all for coming tonight and for opening your hearts and wallets," she said with a wink. "All jokes aside, tonight, we've auctioned off some of the city's finest items—art, jewelry, and artifacts—raising an awe-inspiring three and a half million dollars. All of the proceeds tonight will go to building homes for single mothers and their children, a cause that means a lot to Ryker and me."

The crowd applauded politely.

"The night is not over. We have one more special surprise for the man himself, Ryker Alfero, who's late for his own gala." She scowled, and the crowd laughed. "He's going to kill me for telling you this . . . but his birthday was a couple days ago."

The crowd clapped, and she quieted them down.

Rosa continued. "Now, now, settle down. The big, bad alpha hasn't celebrated his birthday in years, but tonight"—she winked at me—"I have a special surprise for him. So keep drinking and stick around, and we'll present it once he arrives."

The music started again, and Rosa left the stage.

I took a sip of my martini, annoyed with Ryker for being late. *How could he be late for his own charity event?* Given his track record, he might not even show up at all. Rumor was he hated these events but threw them as a way to raise money for his favorite charities and give Others something productive to do besides fighting over territory, power, and women.

I smiled when I caught sight of Sophie coming straight toward me. I knew this bickering and arguing with her had to stop. It had been amusing when I had no intention of going after Ryker. Now that I'd decided to make him mine, things had changed. I had to put an end to Sophie's antics.

Let the games begin.

Sophie stood within inches of me, using her height as intimidation. I definitely disliked her. My body appeared languid, but inside, I was prepared for anything from the viper.

Up close, I had to admit the woman was beautiful. Her hair was a mass of spun gold perfection, and her porcelain skin was flawless. But that was only outer beauty. I could tell by the cold look in her blue eyes and the way her lip curled upward into an icy smile that Sophie was ugly and evil on the inside.

"You actually think you snared the alpha?" she questioned.

"Go away, Sophie," I snapped.

Sophie tossed her hair over her shoulder. "You're pretty. I'll give you that much, but I've heard things about you, nasty things," she sneered. "A fae witch party girl is not exactly mating material and damn sure not fit to be alpha female of the strongest pack in New York."

I arched a brow. "And I presume you are?"

"That's a given," Sophie responded with a smug look.

I shook my head. "Girl, you're aiming way too high."

I sipped my martini and waved at Rosa, who seemed to have some man thoroughly engrossed. Rosa grinned at me, darting her eyes to the man, indicating he was the wolf-shifter she was after. I gave her a thumbs-up.

Sophie glared at Rosa. Rosa stuck up her middle finger at her. I laughed loudly. I guessed I wasn't the only one who despised Sophie.

Sophie smiled. "He hasn't mated for a reason."

I sneered. "Yeah, because he's smart enough not to confuse a one-night stand with a woman he'd actually mate," I spit loudly enough so the surrounding guests heard me.

I was tired of Sophie. Ryker didn't want her, but she refused to go away gracefully.

SOPHIE SPUTTERED WITH HER EYES SELF-CONSCIOUSLY glancing around. "How dare you! He'll never mate a second-rate fae witch, and I'm not going to stand by while you steal him away." She finished.

God, this psycho is tenacious and crazy. But I had learned something. She was socially conscious, which was like waving a red flag at a bull. I would send her packing in shame.

I dramatically batted my eyes. "Watch me. Look, I'm done playing around with you. So here's what you're going to do. You're going to back away from Ryker, because he's mine. That's it. End of fucking story."

Sophie stepped closer. "How about I shift and then fucking tear your ass into so many pieces Ryker won't even recognize you?"

I had enough. Bickering was one thing, but threatening to kill me? She'd crossed the damn line of no return.

"What did you say?" My voice was barely audible.

Her eyes were icy. "I said I will rip you to shreds. Am I clear enough, bitch?"

My hands clenched. "Okay, here's how this shit is going down. The next time I see you and you even flinch at me"—I glared at her—"I'm going to jump up and Superman punch you in the fucking face. No words. Just fucking beat the living shit out of you." I finished, my voice full of menace.

Sophie took a step back.

I was seething with rage. "In fact, the only thing keeping me from cunt-punting your ass across this room is I don't want blood on my fucking couture dress," I sneered. "Now I advise you to walk away before I change my damn mind and show you exactly what a fae witch can actually do."

Sophie sputtered. "This is not the end of this," she spit before stomping away like I'd stolen her fucking bike.

"What did the she-wolf from hell want?" Rosa chirped.

Startled, I looked at her with wide eyes. "God, you're like some type of crazy ninja. You need to wear a freaking bell."

"Ryker's not interested in her." Rosa assured.

I frowned. "Never mind all that. Why the hell didn't you tell me earlier that you were planning a birthday surprise for Ryker?"

She shrugged with a not-too-innocent look on her face. "He doesn't celebrate it . . . ever." She smugly watched me. "Now he has a reason and a person to celebrate it with—you."

"Uh-huh." I warily observed her, waiting for the other shoe to drop.

Her eyes shifted away from me.

I suspiciously eyed her. "What are you up to, Rosa?"

"Nothing. I need you to help me set up his present, which is waiting backstage."

"Uh-huh." I paused. "And you couldn't tell me this earlier because . . . ?"

She wrapped her arm around my waist, dragging me through the crowd. "Never mind that. You're a size nine, right?"

"Yes. What the hell are you up to, Rosa?" I requested when we stepped backstage. I skidded to a stop when I saw the giant white birthday cake.

She sheepishly regarded me. "I was tired of watching you two dance around each other."

I walked around the cake. "You want me to jump out of this thing, huh?"

She pointed over to an outfit hanging on a garment rack—a stunning pinup-style, strapless corset, black satin dress with attached garters. "Wearing this, of course." She apprehensively studied me. "It's for his birthday, sweetie."

Without pause, I kicked off my stilettos. "That's all you had to say, Rosa." I winked at her. "Next time, give a girl some warning." I examined the skimpiness of the figure-flattering dress with light boning, a zipper front, and full lace-up back. "Lucky I shaved, because this dress is bordering on Brazilian wax territory, but I'll make it work."

Rosa tightly hugged me. "I knew you would do it for him."

I smiled impishly. "Who said I'm doing this for him? I haven't gotten laid in months. One look at me in this outfit, and the alpha's definitely going to do me in the back of the limo." I shivered deliciously. "Shit, I'm getting turned on already."

"God, you're truly hilarious." Rosa hugged me again. "You and Ryker will be happy together."

I hugged her back. "Yeah, yeah, yeah. Where are my matching fuck-me shoes?"

She pointed to a pair of sparkling black heels tucked in the corner as I started to unzip my dress.

"You are not getting into that cake," Sophie screeched.

I tilted my head, staring at Sophie, who was practically foaming at the mouth.

Rosa blocked her. "There's only one person going into that damn cake. And that's Light," she snapped.

"Not if she's dead," Sophie boasted while kicking off her shoes.

"Rosa, please step aside," I warned coldly. "You and I know she won't stop if I don't deal with this right now."

It was the way of the shifters. They preyed on the weak, and if I didn't make a stand now, Sophie would make a point to challenge me at every opportunity. I couldn't continue to deal with Sophie as a distraction to Ryker's pack or his position as leader of the council. Besides, if I was going to be alpha female, I had to take a hard stance. There was no other way. And even though I abhorred catfights in any form, this stance was absolutely necessary.

Rosa sighed heavily before stepping aside. "Fine." She looked at Sophie. "But you can't shift."

I headed toward the center of the floor, all the while watching Sophie. She hadn't budged and was glaring at me. She slowly stepped forward with a wide grin on her face. Moments later, she launched herself at me, and I quickly shifted out of the way. Sophie stumbled forward, rolling into a crouch. Before I could turn, she jumped once more as I dodged her.

Sophie growled, cracking her neck, "When I'm done with you, Ryker won't recognize that pretty face."

My hands clenched. My body hummed. "I've been waiting for days to kick your ass, bitch."

That should have been the first clue that things were going to get real nasty. I hurled myself at her and flipped her onto her back. Our gowns ripped. I began choking her without mercy, enjoying watching her struggle for air, as she scratched at my arms. Despite the pain, I felt something dark slithering within me, taking control. My pulse raced as I stood, dragging Sophie by the throat, lifting her, until her feet dangled like a rag doll. Sophie continued to scratch, but I wouldn't let go. I couldn't. My hold on her neck tightened. The darkness urged me to kill her.

"Do you give up?" I hissed.

Sophie stopped struggling and went limp.

I grunted, releasing my grip, thinking it was over. Sophie lifted her knee hard, catching me in the belly. I doubled over. When I straightened, Sophie looked at me with deadly intent and charged at me. I didn't think. I acted. I let the darkness engulf me. My fingers tingled as I lifted my hand, blasting her back onto her ass. She slowly got up and stared at me with disbelief. Her breathing was labored as she circled me, while I hadn't broken a sweat.

Sophie clawed at her dress, trying to get it off. She was attempting to shift. I blew her back. This time, the explosion sent her flying into the wall with a crunch. I slowly stalked toward her.

Kill her. Just kill her, the voice echoed in my head.

Sophie sought to stand up but collapsed to her knees. I read the panic in her eyes, but I didn't care. I wanted her dead.

Kill her, the voice urged again.

I stopped midstride as Sophie looked at me with terror.

"Mercy," she hissed.

I stepped back, struggling to roll the power away. Sophie looked at me with lowered eyes as she backed away. I didn't have to speak. I saw the grudging respect in her eyes before she slinked away.

I felt a hand on my shoulder.

It was Rosa's gentle hand. "Does he know about your power?"

My body tensed. "Not everything."

Rosa turned me to face her. "Trust him with the truth."

I nodded. She smiled, pulling the damp strands of hair away from my forehead.

"Rosa, he's here," her assistant babbled from the entryway.

"Do you still want to do this?" Rosa asked.

I composed myself. "More than anything."

"That's my girl. Get dressed. Your alpha is awaiting his birthday cake."

❧ 21 ❧

LIGHTNING

As I remained inside the giant birthday cake, I refused to let doubt and fear taint my decision to tell Ryker the truth about what I was. We would work on this together. I was a fighter. I wouldn't slink away. Life was too short.

I felt the cake move onto the stage, and I waited anxiously for the cue to jump out.

Rosa whistled. "There he is—the birthday boy!" she screamed.

The birthday music started.

I laughed because I could practically hear the grinding of his teeth.

"Ryker. Wipe that scowl from your handsome face. Come on. Wave, Ryker, so everyone can see you." Rosa chuckled. "Did you just give me the one-finger salute? Not nice, Ryker Alfero." The guests burst out with laughter before Rosa cried, "Oh, isn't he handsome?" I heard clapping and whistling. "By the way, he's no longer single, ladies."

I had to admit she was hilarious. The crowd loved Rosa, and so did I. This was turning out to be the most fun I'd had in a long time.

I waited patiently for the music to stop. My stomach did flip-flops when the last note ended.

Well, it's now or never. I popped up from the cake.

Others' eyebrows rose. Women's mouths dropped open with shock. Some openly looked at me with hate. More than a few whispered with surprise.

The crowd actually parted like the Red Sea as Ryker bulldozed through the guests with a neutral look on his face. He stopped mere inches from the stage. While he watched me with delicious intensity, I immediately became all hot and jittery.

Ryker's brows furrowed. He was waiting for the words he needed. From the determined look on his face, I knew it was all or nothing. There was a fluttery feeling in my chest, but I was unwavering with my decision to give him all of me, knowing my life with him wouldn't be easy. He would challenge me to be greater, as I would expect the same from him. But I knew, without a doubt, he would love me, no holds barred.

I stared at him. "I'm yours—mind, body, and soul." My muscles tightened in readiness.

He blankly looked at me before his lips curled up into a kick-ass grin. "About fucking time!" He leaped onto the stage and tried to haul me out of the cake. "Now we go home, and I mate you properly," he roared. "I can't even count the ways I'm going to wear your ass out tonight."

I pushed him away. "Words . . . let me have them"—I glared —"now."

He grabbed the back of my hair and held me still. "I belong to you—mind, body, and soul. And now that you're mine, I'm never letting go."

Ryker arched into my body as he sucked my tongue into his mouth. My tongue slid around the tip of his and then rubbed under it. He let his hands slip downward to my neck and then slid against my body to my hips. He swooped down and kissed my throat.

I turned my head, but not fast enough to hide my smile. "Okay, alpha, let's go home and fuck already."

He growled before hauling me over his shoulder, jumping off the stage, and plowing through the crowd like a man on a mission as the guests clapped and whistled boisterously.

~

I GLARED AT BONES. "BONES? CAN YOU DRIVE FASTER?" I TOED Ryker's cock with the tip of my shoe as I lay across the backseat.

"We need to talk," Ryker announced gruffly.

My eyes glittered with frustration. "Now? I'm really horny. Can't we talk after?"

"No. I don't want any secrets between us when I claim you."

A long moment passed before anyone spoke.

"I'm sorry." I sighed. "I shouldn't have kept secrets about my sperm donor."

"It's who you are. You don't let people in. I've had to scratch and claw for every inch."

"Ryker—"

"Please let me finish."

I stayed silent.

"I'm not caving on this, Light. You give us a fair chance, and all the pieces will fall into place."

My breathing accelerated, bracing for the impact of telling him the truth. "A romantic. Who would have thought?" I mumbled, still hedging the impending conversation.

He shrugged. "Not romantic. Realistic. If I wanted sex, I could get it anywhere. I've lived a long time, and it gets real empty, but finding that connection"—he tilted my chin—"that's worth the wait. You're worth the wait." He paused. "I know who you are, Light. You hide yourself with men who have no chance in hell of getting your heart or loving you."

I bit my bottom lip. "I'm a hard woman, Ryker. What man would take the risk of loving me?"

"Me. Let me in."

I licked my suddenly dry lips. "I'm an empath, the only true empath within the Credence bloodline." I paused. "Thanks to my mother procreating with the son of the leader of the Shadows." I shrugged, trying not to fidget nervously. "Apparently, this empath crap is important to the Shadows. That's why they want me."

He stared at me. "Empath?"

"Yeah, empaths are—"

"I know what empaths are, but what does this have to do with us?"

"Let me finish. I have been cursed with the ability to sense human emotions—fear, lust, anger. Well, you get the picture."

"Sounds annoying," he murmured.

"More painful, if anything. The constant barrage of emotions starts to cloy at my insides. Sometimes, I can't tell my emotions from the humans' influx of emotions. Anyway, I've tried everything to wall their emotions from me. Nothing truly worked. Alcohol dulled the impact for a while. Connecting mentally with Storm temporarily soothed it. Then this annoying wolf-shifter walked into my life." I sheepishly looked at him. "And that was a game changer." I shrugged. "Don't ask me how, but it did."

His eyes narrowed. "I knew something was different about you. When we met with the detective, it was like I could feel your pain, your anxiety, but I told myself I was imagining things."

My lips trembled. "You weren't. I felt the relief from the symptoms the second you touched me. It was freaky, but I didn't care. It worked." I paused. "I want you to know what you're getting into when you claim me. You and I know it's a matter of time before this shit with the Shadows hits the fan, and the council and Others will know my connection. It's bad enough that they refuse to accept a fae witch, but now I've got three strikes against me. I'm a hybrid, I'm a dysfunctional empath, and my sperm donor and his father are a bunch of raving lunatics."

"I don't care, Light. Nothing about your bloodline, family, or history will change my mind about wanting you."

I looked up, watching Bones, who was driving and no doubt eavesdropping. "And your pack? Do they feel the same way?"

If I accepted Ryker's claim, I would be the alpha female of the pack, second to Ryker. Wolf-shifters didn't give respect because of position; you had to earn it.

Ryker laughed loudly. "The pack fucking loves you. If I had to hear them rib me one more time about claiming you or they would, I would have fucking broken all their necks."

Bones cleared his throat. "We voted you alpha female days ago."

I smiled, trying not to get all emotional over their acceptance. I thought about the Shadows attempt to kidnap me at Redemption. I knew it wouldn't be the Shadows last effort.

Could I risk Ryker's life? What about the pack?

Ryker ran a finger across my cheek. "Stay in the present, baby. Let me worry about the future."

There was a quiver in my stomach. He calmed me, completed me, and scared the living shit out of me.

"There's no other woman for me. And there's no other man for you."

I smirked. "But if you think I'm going to turn into one of those simpering women who bows to her mate after being claimed, then you have another thing coming, alpha."

He growled impatiently. "The only bowing I want is in our bedroom—with you on your knees and my cock down your throat."

I seriously looked at him. "I'll always struggle with this empath shit. You might have cured the pain and the crazy, but you can't protect me from having to deal with humans and their emotions."

"It won't be easy, but with our mating, your control will only get better."

"Maybe."

He scowled. "When are you going to realize that we're better together than apart? I'm not looking to change you. I love you the way you are."

I didn't blink when, in a roundabout way, he'd admitted to loving me. For Others, we connected on a whole different level. Our feelings were pure, quick, and raw, with no games.

I smiled impishly. "Wow, the alpha loves me, warts and all."

He growled, "Damn right, woman."

"Good, because I've decided to keep your angry, psychotic ass." I nipped his bottom lip.

"Really? Decided? You had no choice, woman. Now let's get the formalities out of the way. You belong to me and no other. And I belong to you. I haven't touched or looked at another woman since the first charity gala."

I frowned. "Better not have."

"There's no other woman for me. I'm a mean SOB sometimes, but you'll deal, like I can deal with your crazier-than-hell mood swings."

I grinned. "Oh, fuck off, alpha. I'm not moody. I'm eccentric."

He arched a brow.

"Well, I am."

"Know that after I claim you, you'll be alpha female of this dysfunctional pack, and there's a shitload of work we need to do to get this pack functional." He kissed me with a passion, which took my breath away. "I know we can do it—together."

I grabbed his penis. "Don't I get to sample the goods before I sign up for duty, sir?" I smiled widely. "I don't want to be stuck with some alpha who can't turn me out on a nightly basis. I want sex . . . and lots of it."

He smiled sexily. "When I get you on all fours, I plan on making your toes curl."

A tremor went through my body as my cunt contracted. "I love that, baby. Aim high."

I ran my tongue over his firm lips. I had let go of the fear. He was the man for me, the man who destroyed the madness and fright.

"And for the record, I accept everything you're offering, alpha." I grabbed his hair. "There's no other man like you. I know this . . . and I'll love your insane ass forever."

His eyes softened. "Well, well, well, Lightning Credence has finally admitted she loves me. Be still my fucking heart."

"Don't get all cocky, but I'm wildly turned on right now." I ran my palm against his powerfully built thigh.

He regarded me with half-open eyes. "Like, how turned on?" he demanded with a gruff voice.

I couldn't help but think about how desperately I wanted him. I stared at him, wondering how the hell this shit had happened.

"Like, on-my-knees hot," I blurted out without blinking. There was no shame in my game. I always asked for what I wanted. And I wanted him—now. I ran a hand across his crotch and winked. "Let the fucking commence. It's been a while, and I plan on keeping you up all night."

Bones, eavesdropping, nervously jerked the wheel, trying not to crash. "Holy shit!"

Ryker rolled up the partition before his eyes locked onto mine. I licked my bottom lip with anticipation. He grabbed my thigh, draping it over his brawny leg, leaving me wide open. The cold air brushed against my womanhood as he slid a hand between my legs, pinching my clit. My lips parted.

"Harder," I whispered.

Bones smoothly pulled into the underground parking garage and parked.

Ryker rolled down the partition. "Bones, step out of the car. I don't need you seeing Lightning on her knees." He squeezed my thigh hard and then soothingly rubbed it.

Bones smoothly hopped out of the car. "I'm going to need a cold shower," he mumbled under his breath as he walked away.

"Ready to fuck, alpha?" I pushed up the hem of my dress, straddling his legs. I slowly shook my hair as I rotated my hips.

He grabbed my ass, hard, stilling my movement. I knew handprints would be all over my ass, but I didn't give a shit. Right now, I wanted him. I licked his lips, unzipped his pants, and grabbed his cock.

"Impressive." I bit his lower lip. "I want you . . . now . . ."

THE SULTRINESS OF THE AIR SKIMMED ACROSS MY SKIN. ALL the fun and games were over. This was the truth. There was no compromising. His eyes flashed gold. They were now more wolf-like than human. He was letting his wolf slowly out of the cage, seeing if I would hightail it out of the vehicle. But that shit wasn't going to happen. I wasn't that girl. I was sticking around.

"I'm never letting you go," he growled.

I reached up, digging my fingers into his hair, scratching my nails across his scalp. He growled with a rumbling reverberation in his wide chest. He was showing me the real him—the man, the wolf, a part of him he usually kept leashed to prevent the beast from taking over and sending him feral.

He continued. "This will never work until you trust me, giving me your submission. You must surrender your heart, body, and soul, as I am willing to do for you. Trust is the only thing that can keep us together. I trust that you accept the man I am. And you need to trust my acceptance of the woman you keep hidden."

I calmed my breathing.

He'd stripped away my mask, leaving me bare, vulnerable, and raw. For the first time in my life, I would have a protective, caring man who would cherish me for as long as I allowed it. And I wanted forever.

"And what if the woman you think I am isn't there?" I paused. "I'm more than what you see."

"That's what I'm counting on. Nothing is perfect. I'm far

from it, but I'm half the man without you." He grabbed my face between his calloused hands. "On your knees, darling—now." He tipped his head in a wolf-like way. "Submit to your alpha." His voice was hard and unyielding.

"Submission," I whispered, as if rolling the word over my tongue like a fine wine. "And do you think you've earned my submission?"

"Make no mistake about it." His eyes were almost savage. His canines dropped. "I'm wild and ruthless, and I don't give a shit about anything but what belongs to me—you."

Adrenaline rushed through my body.

I wanted the freedom of not having to think every second. He was giving me that independence. After spending a lifetime of overthinking everything in my life, it was liberating to put my trust in his hands. Submission wasn't about being weak. It wasn't designed to make a submissive feel powerless. That was the misconception about D/s relationships. It was part of the power dynamics. The truth of the matter was sexual submissives had all the power in the relationship.

He gripped my hair, sloping my head back. I knew what he wanted. It wasn't about sex . . . not anymore. It was about sharing a piece of me I had long buried away, a part of me that needed nurturing, love, and acceptance. I knew he wouldn't push or force. He would wait for me to submit—not because it was what he wanted, but because it was what I wanted to give. That piece of me was reserved and owned only by him.

I tilted my head in submission. His body tensed as his wolf receded; his eyes were now more human. I wrapped my hands around his penis and squeezed hard. He hissed as he relaxed against the soft leather. There was no need for words. He knew I was meeting him halfway, revealing a part of me who was better left hidden. I lowered the walls around my mind as I slid to my knees. He stopped me by grabbing the back of my neck and pulling hard on my hair.

"I want you." I trailed my fingers over his chest.

With locked eyes, he asked hoarsely, "Are you mine?"

"Always."

He pulled me up. "Good." He slammed open the vehicle door, stepping out. "Now get your sexy ass out of the car."

He grasped my hand as I hurriedly hopped out, straightening my dress. He leaned down, kissing me. With our tongues dueling, I ran my fingers across the hard muscles of his back.

He pulled back, looking at the one visible security camera. "Soar, cut off the security cameras."

I hadn't even thought about the number of security cameras monitoring the garage area. That was how far gone I was.

Effortlessly, he slid me onto the hood of the car, pushing my dress up around my waist.

"Well . . . I thought we'd finish this upstairs. But I'm down for whatev—" I swallowed the rest of my words when I found myself on my back with my legs up over his shoulders and his face between my thighs.

He voraciously went after my pussy, his abrasive tongue lapping me from my clit to the end of my cleft. I panted, my hips arching before he held me down with one hand on my stomach. He snarled. The vibrations pushed me to the edge. His long strokes had me writhing, my fingers clawing the car as I tried to move from his tongue assault.

He pinned me, showing me no damn mercy, as his tongue flicked my swollen nub until I screamed.

"Oh my fucking God." I bucked as he continued to bathe my clit with his mouth.

He thrust two fingers into my trembling channel, pumping me, drawing out my climax. My eyes rolled to the back of my head, and I swore I saw dancing spots. I panted, drawing ragged breaths. Mercifully, he relented, pulling away, his eyes blazing with wildness and his black hair tousled sexily. I was greedy for more.

Holy hell, I couldn't even form a coherent thought. "Fuck me," I demanded.

He growled, his expression more beast than man. "I'll give you five minutes to get upstairs"—he ran a calloused thumb over my bottom lip—"where you'll show me all the things your sexy mouth and sinful body promise."

He lifted me off the car and securely held me as my legs wobbled, my body a shuddering mass of jelly.

He softly kissed me on the lips. "You okay, darling? You look a little . . . dazed."

"Not dazed . . . fucking amazed. Believe me; that's not easy to do." I smirked while cupping his hard cock. "Wolfie, we are going to do great things together." I wanted him right now.

He slapped my ass. "Off you go, vixen."

"Whatever you want, Ryker." I squeezed it hard, smiling with satisfaction when he hissed. "I'll be waiting, Wolfie," I taunted before turning on my heel and walking away.

I basked in the heat of his gaze as he stared at me all the way to the elevator. Sliding into the elevator, I watched as he leaned against the vehicle with a lit cigar in his mouth. I reached up and unzipped the front of the strapless corset dress, letting it slide down a little, revealing a glimpse of my breasts.

Ryker smiled . . . an honest-to-God naughty boy smile. My heart thumped as the elevator door slid closed.

My pulse raced. I was like a kid in a candy store. I didn't know where to start. *Should he take me on the kitchen counter? Maybe the balcony? The bedroom seems too vanilla for our first time. Yes, definitely the balcony.*

I walked out of the elevator with a bouncy strut, contemplating the ecstasy of finally having him, when I heard his voice from the shadows.

"Strip," he ordered with a hoarse tone. "I want to see all that shit you were talking about in the car."

My eyes tried to adjust to the darkness of the living room. "How the hell did you get up here so fast?"

"Light," he growled impatiently.

I heard soft clicking before the terrace doors slid open,

streaming moonlight over him as he sat on a chair facing me with a remote in his hand. He looked hard, sexy, and in control as he tossed away the device.

I flipped my hair. "Why, Ryker, you've read my mind. I'd love to strip and get raunchy on the terrace." Hell, I was adventurous.

I swayed over to him.

"Strip—right here, right now. I want to see you take off your sexy dress while I watch, thinking about all the dirty things I'm going to do to that sexy body of yours."

I was an exhibitionist by nature, and stripping before him ramped up my adrenaline, making me giddy with lust.

I deliberately circled his chair, giving him my best smoldering gaze while trailing my fingers against his neck. As I passed behind him, I leaned over, brushing my breasts against his back, whispering, "When I first met you, I wanted you to fuck me. Now I'm greedy. I want more. I want you to love me." I ran my tongue along his ear, brushing it across his neck.

He reached up, grabbing the back of my hair, and growled in the sexiest voice I'd ever heard, "I love you not only for what you are, but for what I am when I am with you."

I blinked back the tears of joy. "I love you, too, my sexy alpha." I twirled around him, stopping in front of him. I bent over so he could peek down my dress. I twisted around, placing one foot on the couch and, at a snail's pace, inclined my body from the waist, practically putting my ass in his face. "Do you want to touch it, baby?" My breathing hitched as I felt his fingers run along my ass seam.

"You have the sexiest ass I've ever seen. I can't wait to take you from behind."

I unhurriedly unhooked the garters, pausing to tauntingly wiggle my ass. "You sure you know what to do with all this ass?"

"Tease."

He slapped my ass cheek so hard that I knew I would have a handprint there. I moaned when the delicious zing went straight to my cunt. He rubbed his hand over the cheek, soothing the pain of the sting.

I twirled to face him. "Did I displease you, alpha?" I asked with a flirtatious smile.

"There's nothing your sexy body could do to displease me . . . besides disobey." He sternly looked at me. "Continue to strip."

"What if I don't? Will you punish me?" *Please say yes! Punish me.*

"Take off the dress," Ryker demanded with a hard voice.

I unzipped the corset dress. There was something so intimate and hot as I stared into his eyes while removing my dress before letting it drop at my feet. "Like this?"

He grinned, his teeth flashing white. "Just like that, darling."

Tweaking my nipples to make them erect, I asked him, "Do you like it when my nipples are hard?" I swung my foot up on his shoulder, stroking my womanhood.

"Shit," he groaned. "I didn't realize you were that limber."

I leaned in, licking the shell of his ear. "If only you knew how limber," I whispered.

"If you kiss my neck, it's done. We're fucking," he hissed.

Pushing back, I straddled one of his legs, lowering myself onto it, and then I briefly rubbed my crotch against his thigh, making sure to press on his hard cock, giving him a lap dance. "If you like, you can touch it, baby."

"To hell with taking it slow. I need my cock lodged so deep into your pussy that you can taste it in the back of your throat," he barked with a voice deep and smooth as he sprang up from the chair.

"Do your worst, baby."

Instinctively, I wrapped my legs around his lean waist, digging my heels into his ass as he effortlessly carried me through the penthouse before kicking his bedroom door open like he was the police. Dropping me onto the bed, he straddled me, one knee on each side of my waist. I stared up at him with anticipation. His firm lips curved a little into a smile.

He stroked my hair. "Have you ever been tied, darling?"

"No," I whispered. "I've never trusted anyone enough."

His eyes never left mine as he picked up my hands and lifted them toward the head of the bed, wrapping a soft strap around them. Excitement bubbled up in me as he moved to lie beside me.

He cupped my cheek in one huge hand, forcing me to meet his sensual gaze. "Do you trust me to take care of you?"

I nodded. He brushed a tender kiss across my lips and nuzzled my temple. I lay there, hands tied over my head, as he stood and stripped slowly. His skin was golden tan and tight over the bulging muscles beneath. He was, without a doubt, the sexiest man I'd ever seen . . . and he was all mine.

My eyes dropped lower. His huge erection was thick, hard, and jutting toward me. My mind raced, wondering how the hell he was going to fit all that into me—not that I was going to let his big cock intimidate me. I was determined to ensure every inch got in.

He joined me on the bed. He caressed my cheek before his tongue took full possession, darting in and out of my mouth.

"So beautiful," he murmured with approval as he slid down.

He pressed his mouth against my stomach, nibbling and kissing, until all I wanted to do was burst into flames.

He knelt between my legs, hungrily looking at me. He pushed my leg out a little. Now I was even more exposed and vulnerable before his gaze.

He cupped my pussy. "Knees up to your stomach, darling."

I blinked, bringing my knees up to my stomach. He pressed them outward, tipping my pussy up in the air.

He gazed straight into my eyes. "This is how I always want you—open and ready for whatever I need from you." He slid his fingers between the wet folds of my heat. "This pussy is mine to do with as I please."

I arched up, wiggling closer, as he slipped his fingers inside.

His thumb circled and played with my clit. "Whether it is with my cock or mouth, this pussy is all mine."

I was dying for more even though I was on the brink of my first orgasm. Staring at him, my mind went numb. I needed more but was helpless. He stroked my heat, and I shivered, on the verge of exploding. I knew he had no intention of pushing me over the edge until I said what he needed to hear.

"Please," I whispered. "I just . . . Please . . . lick me."

"Was that so hard, darling?"

His huge hands curled around my thighs, spreading me wider, and his tongue thrust into my heat. That one abrasive lick sent me spiraling over the edge, and I screamed his name like a prayer.

He pulled his head back and watched me as his fingers continued to stretch me. "Scream louder, darling."

I was writhing and panting as my hips bucked wildly. His fingers thrust harder. I moaned louder when his finger found my clit again and mercilessly played with it. I screamed and came again, feeling lightheaded from the passion.

I must have blacked out, because by the time I caught my breath, Ryker was right above me, his weight on his knees between my thighs. He directed his cock into position, smoothly slipping in, as he looked at me with burning possession on his face. I struggled to breathe as his cock stretched me like no other.

He gave me a slow smile. "You are mine," he grunted, fully seated with his balls bumping against my ass.

He kissed my lips, my jaw, and my eyes. I basked in his tenderness and love. He pulled out and sank back in, hitting my G-spot with precision. My legs wrapped around his waist as he continued to hit my G-spot, making my legs quiver. My pussy sucked him in farther as he thrust deeper. My hips tilted forward, and he adjusted his movements so he brushed deliciously against my clit with each stroke. The deeper he pumped, the more I wanted him. My head snapped back as he slid in and out. I writhed beneath him, meeting him thrust for thrust. I was trembling, moaning low and deep.

He stilled my hips so I felt every inch of his pulsing cock.

"It's going to last all night, darling. No rushing," he growled in my ear as he released my arms from the bonds.

I slid my hands over his back, my nails digging into him like I was a wild woman. He continued pumping, hard and methodical.

I was going insane from the heat building. My breathing was fast and shallow, with periods of whimpers intermixed.

"Please . . . harder." I grabbed his head, pulling him closer, biting his lower lip. "Please?"

He let himself go, moving faster, pushing me into another orgasm. Arching, I screamed as my pussy clenched around him. Then I collapsed right after, worn out and sweaty.

His face was harsh and controlled as he pulled from my body, flipping me onto my belly. He pulled me up onto my knees. I moaned when he kissed my neck and shoulders and then rained kisses along my spine. He nudged me forward, onto my hands. His growl was animalistic. The air crackled around us as his strong hands seized my waist, and his cock smoothly thrust into me. I cried out with pleasure as one hand gripped my hair while the other was wrapped around my waist. His body rocked into me. Our bodies, slick with sweat, were in perfect synchrony, with a strange magnetic energy wrapping around us.

"Make me yours . . . completely," I whispered, clutching the bedsheets.

He reared back and pushed forward. Every inch of him was sheathed in me. My body shook, my legs quivered, and my core pulsed, racing toward blissful release.

"Do you accept me as your mate?" he demanded roughly, thrusting faster.

"Yes. Only you, Ryker," I moaned.

"Lightning Credence, you're mine, and what I claim, I keep, cherish, love, and protect."

His thrusts grew stronger as his body slapped against me. My fingers clenched the sheets as I rocked back into his body. My body was burning for a sweet release. A strangled shout escaped his lips before he bit the spot between my neck and shoulder. I came so hard I screamed his name at the top of my lungs. My inner muscles contracted, milking him. He roared, shooting his seed deep into my scorching core, both of us cresting.

He kissed me on my shoulder before pulling me up farther onto the bed. Clutching me against his body, he kissed me, and with my eyes closed, I kissed him back.

There was no going back—not that I wanted to. With every fiber in my body, I knew this man would love me hard and cherish me until his last breath.

I sighed, content, as we held on to each other, lips melding over and over as the tremors passed.

"So I guess you're stuck with me, Wolfie," I sassed, letting out a little laugh.

He nuzzled my neck. "I wouldn't have it any other way," he quipped, nibbling on my ear.

He found the mark he'd left on my shoulder and gently licked it. A shiver shot through my body.

"What is it like to be an empath?"

I sighed, cuddling into his body. "It's like a blackout. When I'm around humans, I don't know what the hell happens. I'm gone. Everything they feel becomes infused into me. It's like my own personal hell."

He raked his fingers through the strands of my hair, calming the turbulent waters of raging emotions. He didn't interrupt. He was my calmness, my strength, and now . . . my rock.

"The crazy thing is, I now know this empath thing is power-ful. I am powerful." I paused. "I'm more powerful than my mind can even digest and understand."

"If you can harness your own power and put it to your own use, well, then there are no limits," he responded.

"Maybe. I'm not there yet." Tracing a finger over the intricate gold and black of a sword tattooed on his forearm, I asked, while staring at the sword's hilt and leaf-shaped brass blade, "What was it like when the goddess of death appeared to you?"

Ryker's eyes darkened. "I've seen a lot in my lifetime, but nothing like her. There weren't a lot of bullshit words. She pointed at me and said it was my time. She didn't ask for permission when she slapped this mark on me, making me the bearer of the Sword of Souls."

"She didn't ask? It seems like a hell of a lot of responsibility to thrust onto someone without even a damn discussion."

He shrugged. "Goddesses don't ask. They tell you what to do, like female sexual Dominants."

I snickered. "It must have been hell for a Dom like you."

He bit my shoulder with a laugh.

"Being born into the Alfero bloodline, didn't you expect to be chosen?" I asked.

He kissed my fingers, one by one. "No. There was only one other bearer in my family, Tiber, and that was centuries ago. He fucked up his responsibilities so bad that the family thought the goddess was done with our bloodline." His eyes turned bleak. "I wouldn't have blamed her if she were.

"Nothing good ever happened to any of the alphas in my family. That's why I couldn't wait to leave when I turned eighteen. I couldn't live the life my father had created for me. And when my mother was killed, shit got worse. He went feral, and with the help of his brother, it was total chaos." He made a low noise in his throat. "I held on for as long as I could because I knew my mother would have expected me to stay by his side, to at least try to help him, but when he made the alliance with the Jenson pack, assuming I would fall in line and mate with Sophie, I knew I had to leave."

I kissed his shoulder. "But you came back."

"I had no choice," he ground out. "I came back because the goddess told me my father had been killed by his brother. That's what she really meant by *it was time*. It was time for me to claim the position of alpha and unite the Others." He shrugged. "I guess I could have refused to come back, but I knew this pack needed me. So I resigned from my position at the hospital and came back."

I saw the sadness in his eyes, and I wanted so badly to take it away. "You mean you came back to chaos."

He absently ran a hand along my hip while staring into space. "Fighting my uncle for the alpha position was an easy decision. The prick deserved to be taken down. It was taking over as the leader of the Other Council that was hard. No one respected the Alfero name. My father and his brother had singlehandedly run the name into the ground. The only thing I had to help me rebuild was the power of the Sword of Souls and the goddess's edict to unite the Others. So I used it to get them in line, forcing the Others into a temporary truce."

"But you really need the peace treaty to happen," I insisted.

"My mission was clear—unite the Others. Frankly, when she ordered it, I didn't think it was remotely possible. Still don't. But I do agree it's the only thing to keep them from killing each other into extinction."

I squeezed his arm. "It can still happen. We'll make this happen."

He smiled. "My alpha female is ready, huh?"

"Oh, so ready." But I knew it wouldn't be easy. "You know, equality among Others is a myth, and for some reason, everyone accepts the fact that women shouldn't hold as much power as men do. I don't understand that. Why do we have to take a backseat?"

It was a big point of frustration for me. It was one thing for men to be dominant inside the bedroom, which I was all for, but outside of it, we were their equivalent.

"Men were given the power to run the show, power to define the value of an alpha female. It's ridiculous. I'm going to shake up their world, starting by taking an active role in getting this treaty to happen. First, we need to stop the Shadows."

He gave me the same sexy smile that always made my toes

curl, before saying, "We will. With you by my side, there's nothing we can't do."

I smiled. "*We*—I like that. Most alphas would be pounding on their chests like cavemen, saying the woman's place was a meek one."

He laughed. "Not all. The smart alphas take alpha females who can hold their own . . . like you."

I smirked. "Good. And don't think I'm popping out any puppies anytime soon." I pointed to my soft stomach and curvy hips. "See all this? Between decadent pastries and hours on the couch, watching reality shows, it takes a lot of damn work to maintain all this gorgeousness."

He slapped my ass hard. "The babies can wait. I want us to spend some quality time together first. Anything else?"

I trailed my fingers across his chest. "Yep, first thing in the morning, I must have coffee, or I'll turn into a raving lunatic."

He laughed. "You're already a raving lunatic."

I slapped his chest. "I get worse. Believe me. Now, you, Wolfie, give me your must-haves."

"Just one. I love to fuck in the morning. So be prepared to assume the position on your knees when you wake up, because I'll be serving a regular dose of hard cock every morning, darling."

I shivered deliciously. "Shit, I think I just came." I rolled away from him, stretching suggestively before I got on all fours. "Like this?"

He slid behind me. "Just like that, darling."

He kissed the side of my neck. I moaned.

"And so we're clear, there will be no other women besides me . . . ever. So take a good look at this cunt, Ryker, because you'll be looking at it for a long time."

He grabbed my hair, pulling me up against his chest. "You are all I've ever wanted or needed," he whispered in my ear.

I grunted with satisfaction. "Better be."

He spun me around to face him. "Now that all the heavy stuff is out of the way, say you love me, Light."

"I love you, Ryker Alfero." I leaned forward, softly kissing him. "I love you," I whispered against his lips.

His mouth trailed to my neck, biting over his mark of possession. "I love you. I'll always love you." He wrapped his arms around my waist and squeezed.

I grabbed his face, biting his lower lip before tracing my tongue along it. "So . . . can we commence fucking now? Because your alpha female needs her dose of cock." I squeezed it hard. "Like, really bad."

He kissed me long and hard before saying, "Get on your knees . . . now."

22

LIGHTNING

I AWOKE to the sun streaming through the floor-to-ceiling windows. I was draped across Ryker like a blanket, completely exhausted from the morning fuck marathon.

When he'd said he loved to make love in the morning, he wasn't kidding. I was amazed at how he'd kept pulling orgasms out of me when I was absolutely sure I was too tired to continue. Even exhaustion hadn't stopped me from screaming out from pleasure when he expertly pushed me over the edge again and again.

I didn't even have time to kiss him before he pushed into my moist heat, taking me again. I absolutely loved the fuck marathon.

He slapped my ass, rolling me over. "Bath time," he growled.

He lustfully kissed me before jumping up and heading for the bathroom. I listened to the water running, too exhausted to move, when the earthy scent of sandalwood and rosewood wafted into the room. I groaned. Every muscle in my body was blissfully sore. I smiled, thinking about him. I had it bad. The man never seemed to get enough; his cock hadn't gone down for more than a few minutes.

A little while later, he came back into the bedroom, hauling me up and over his shoulder.

"Leave me the hell alone," I groaned, half asleep.

"Nope. We have a busy morning. First, a nice, warm bath. Next, I make my mate breakfast. Finally, we're going to your house for a meeting with Ava and Lia to discuss our new intel."

"Why can't we have breakfast in bed and do a video conference?" I grumbled.

I must have nodded off for a second, because the next thing I knew, I was being dropped into the oversized, deep soaking tub. Ryker climbed in behind me, pulling me against his chest. I sighed as the combination of the hot water and the heady scent of sandalwood and rosewood bath salts cocooned us.

"You're a keeper, Wolfie," I whispered, relaxing against him.

"We're not staying in long. I want to ease your sore muscles."

"Uh-huh," I groaned sleepily.

I dozed off and awoke to being pulled out of the water and pushed into a steamy shower. I didn't even attempt to move when he started washing me.

He laughed. "You're not even going to participate?" he questioned while thoroughly soaping every inch of me.

I yawned. "Nope, you got it covered."

He knelt down to wash my legs and feet and then circled behind me to wash my ass. I couldn't help myself; I grinned and pushed my ass in his face. He bit it hard.

I sharply pulled back. "Did I just feel your canines on my ass?"

"Quiet. I'm working here," he grunted while pushing to his feet. He washed my back and hair.

I popped open an eyelid. "Is it my turn?" I reached for the soap.

He sat me down on the boulder rock seat. "Sit here and be quiet, darling."

I watched languidly as he made quick work of soaping himself. Ryker's body and face were works of art. The only thing that marred his brooding dark face was the scar across his left eyebrow.

"How did you get that scar?" I inquired.

"When I was kicking my uncle's ass, he cut me," he replied gruffly.

"I thought shifters healed quickly."

"We do. I think he cut me with a knife laced with dark magic—a fact he vehemently denied, of course."

I never had the displeasure of meeting his uncle, but I already hated the asshole.

He pulled us both out of the shower, dried us off, and picked me up, marching to his bed.

I rolled over, staring at him. "Am I supposed to be this tired?"

Granted, we'd fucked like rabbits, but I felt unusually tired.

I reached up and scratched the bite mark on my shoulder. "And my shoulder feels funny."

It was like tiny pins were being inserted into the skin over and over again.

His eyes flashed as he ran his fingers along my shoulder, easing the stinging. "Everything is fine, Light."

I rolled over, pressing my face into the pillow. "I need a fifteen-minute nap, and I'll be good to go."

He kissed my back. "Fifteen minutes only. Then I'm coming to get you."

"Uh-huh," I responded, practically knocked out when I heard the door close.

I MOVED OVER ONTO MY BACK, STARING AT THE CEILING. THE nap was longer than the promised fifteen minutes, but I'd needed it. At least Ryker had let me sleep. He probably felt sorry about wearing my ass out.

I rolled out of bed and padded over to my room to dress. Quickly, I pulled on the mesh bralette and a classic sleeveless racerback tank, and I teamed it with cigarette jeans and a pair of front-zip lug-sole booties.

Stepping into the bathroom, I washed my face and nearly choked when I saw two angry-looking red swirls marked onto my skin like a tattoo, right over Ryker's bite. I rubbed it to see if it was an infection—no oozing, just a slight tingle.

I stopped to think. I was going to kill him. He had seen the marks and hadn't had the decency to tell me. Angrily, I pulled my hair into a high ponytail, leaving the room in a huff.

"Ryker, you have some explaining to do. What the hell is this mark on my shoulder?" I skidded to a stop when I saw the whole pack staring at me.

I pointed to the mark. "Is this normal? Because it sure as hell doesn't look normal."

Jackal loudly sniffed the air.

I stared at him. "What?"

He took a step forward and then stopped. "You smell different."

"I took a shower, guys," I huffed.

Rip's head tilted to one side. "No, it's not that. Your scent's changed. You smell like"—he sniffed—"a mixture of Ryker's scent and something else."

Damn these shifters and their keen sense of smell. "So what you're really telling me is I stink?"

Soar leaned against the granite kitchen counter. "Quite the opposite. It's alluring."

Ryker stroked his beard. "Too alluring."

I worriedly looked at Ryker. "Alluring? Alluring, as in shifters following me around, trying to sniff my ass?" I snapped.

Rip edged closer to me.

Ryker's head snapped in his direction, growling warningly.

Rip sheepishly looked at him, stepping back. "Sorry."

"Trouble," Soar noted. He looked over at Ryker. "Maybe it's some fae witch thing."

I pushed my T-shirt strap aside. "What about this mark on my shoulder?" My eyes narrowed.

All of them stared at me as if they had discovered a new species in the wild.

Soar stepped forward. "I've never seen a mate mark quite like that."

I looked at Ryker. "And what about you, Ryker?"

He shrugged. "Never. But I wouldn't worry about it."

I looked at him like he had lost his mind. "There is a mark on my shoulder that wasn't there last night, and you want to ignore it?" I tapped my chin. "Uh, right . . ." I rolled my eyes and pointed at Jackal. "You, geek guy wrapped in the body of a male model, find out what the hell this is. Look in the Others search engine or something."

He laughed. "And what keywords should I enter, oh wise one? *Fae witch fucked an alpha?*"

I threw my hands in the air. "Now everyone thinks they're a comedian." My lips twitched into a smile. "Forget it. You're right. This is unexplainable."

Soar gulped his coffee. "Exactly. Unexplainable. We're shifters who transform into wolves. Try and explain that logically."

"Okay, so riddle me this, shifter. Why do I feel like this is a big deal?"

Ryker softly kissed me. "Because it probably is. That's why when I'm not around, the pack will protect you."

He was acting nonchalant, but I knew it wasn't that simple.

"So let me get this straight. I'm supposed to live my life under twenty-four-seven protection?" I asked.

"Until we eliminate the threat. Stop worrying. Get your ass over here." Ryker pulled out the stool.

"And what about my job?" I demanded as I sat down.

I wasn't stupid. I knew things had changed. I wasn't only the mate of an alpha shifter, but I was also the mate of the most respected and hated Other in North America. There was bound to be some issues from Others trying to hurt him by using me, and I couldn't risk that happening.

"When the council reinstates Credence O., you go back to work." His mouth smashed down onto mine. He pulled back, trailing a finger across my lips. "I'm not trying to change you, Light. But you'll always have security. That shit is not negotiable."

I was happy that we weren't going to have an ugly argument about me working, because I wasn't ever going to step back from working at Credence O. Storm and I had worked hard for our business stake in the company, and I refused to walk away from something I loved. And besides, I truly believed women should be financially independent from their men.

I sighed heavily. "We'll work on the logistics of making this work without putting me in solitary confinement."

He smiled. "I'm one lucky shifter," he drawled.

"And don't you forget it," I responded before he pushed a steaming cup of espresso across the counter. I rubbed my hand across his cheek. "My man remembered. That's earned you one hot and heavy session of me on my knees, blowing your mind."

He winked. "I can't wait," he responded before swinging me away from the breathtaking Central Park view. "Now let me cook my woman some breakfast."

I sat there in awe, watching him bustle around, while he chopped vegetables and stirred things around in the pan, all confident and sure-like. I fucking loved to watch him cook. I was so hot and bothered that all I wanted to do was rip off his clothes and have my filthy way with him right there on the granite counter.

As if he could sense my thoughts, he froze, looking over his shoulder with a sexy smile. And that was all I needed. I hopped off the stool as he turned around, watching my approach with predator eyes, making my heart race with excitement.

Stopping right before him, I stepped between his legs and grabbed his hips, reaching up to lick his silky warm lips. I pushed into his mouth with a persistent tongue. He squeezed my ass with one hand while the other was possessively wrapped around my waist. I almost came when he sucked my tongue into his mouth, twining around it. He plundered and nipped. He growled, a sound that rumbled deep in his chest, as he hoisted me up, kneading my ass with two hands. Instinctively, I wrapped my legs around his waist. I was completely gone. I wanted him right now.

He pulled back with a husky, "We'll finish this later." He softly kissed me before effortlessly carrying me back to the stool.

Jackal stared with his tablet dangling precariously from his fingers. "Holy shit! That was fucking hot."

Rip sheepishly shifted away from the counter, trying to hide his obvious hard-on.

I winked. "Don't be embarrassed. It was definitely a cigars-on-ice moment."

Rip scoffed. "I'm not embarrassed. I'm pissed that I don't have time to take a cold shower to relieve my hard-on."

Jackal shook his head. "See? This is what happens when you don't get laid on a regular basis—a lifetime of embarrassing cigars-on-ice moments."

Annoyed by his attitude, Rip scowled. "Shut up. I wouldn't be bragging when you're secretly lusting after a hybrid vampire."

Jackal slammed his cup onto the table. "I don't do vampires."

Rip grabbed a plate piled high with bacon and eggs, looking at Jackal. "Yeah, that's why you were growling at anyone who even blinked at her. Bullshit."

"Hold on, no one talks about my best friend like that," I snapped.

Ryker slid a plate with a fluffy omelet in front of me. "Eat, baby." He glared at Jackal. "Don't set her off. She's the calmest I've seen her in days."

"I'm not done with you." I dug my fork into the omelet, giving Jackal the evil eye. The first bite melted in my mouth. "Oh. My. God. This is the tastiest thing I've ever eaten."

Ryker growled playfully.

I winked at him. "Besides you, baby."

I continued eating as they piled plates high with food and dug in. I had to admit the vibe was relaxed, like a real family, and I loved it.

I pointed my fork at Rip. "Hey, where's Bones?"

He snarled, "Having a conversation with his former mentor, Noah."

"Conversation?" I took a sip of espresso. "Is that code for kicking his ass?"

He glanced at Ryker.

"No, that's code for having a civil conversation before we have to drag his ass in by force," Ryker responded with a hard voice.

"Hmm." I chewed. "Any attempts to attack the gala last night?"

Soar's face tightened. "No. Apparently, they were warned by a snitch that we were waiting and had prepared for them."

I watched Ryker shake his head at Soar. My eyes narrowed. Something was going on within the pack that had everyone on edge.

"You know, there might be an easier way to get information about the Shadows." My eyes slid to Ryker and then back to the pack.

Ryker pushed his plate away. "No."

Rip looked at him. "No to what?"

I shrugged. "I'm just saying—"

"The answer is still no. You are not contacting your father."

I stared at him, annoyed. "Sperm donor. He's not my father. You know, the crazy thing is I think I've seen him before. I can't remember where."

Rip grunted. "Of course you've seen him before. He pretty much admitted he's been stalking you since you were born."

I shivered. "Okay, the way you put it sounds creepy."

"Because it is," Jackal interjected. "And your grandfather sending men to kidnap you is even creepier."

Ryker got up with his plate. "We don't need him. Your mom found a lead on the missing client list."

"Good. So after we eat, we'll head over there." I swallowed another morsel of food. I was ravenous.

Soar's cell rang, but he continued shoveling food into his mouth. "No, that's great." He hung up. "We got the location of the Shadows' hideout."

"I'm done eating. Let me get my bag, and we'll roll." I pushed away from the counter.

Ryker grabbed my face. "Forget about contacting your father. Ever," he stated flatly.

I cupped his cheek. "Baby, I don't take orders. Now ask nicely."

"Don't fucking try to find him," he growled. "Is that nice enough?"

I smiled sweetly . . . too sweetly. He glared.

"We'll work on your manners later. Many of the most valuable etiquette lessons can be learned under the guidance of my mouth on your cock." I turned on my heel, swaggering away. I was so done discussing this.

RYKER GLANCED INTO THE REARVIEW MIRROR, MAKING SURE the SUV trailing us with Jackal, Rip, and Soar was still behind us, while I sat silently fuming. He placed a hand on my thigh. I glared, pushing his hand off.

Ryker sighed. "Still angry with me, I see."

I incredulously looked at him. "I've been sitting here in I-don't-give-a-shit mode for eleven minutes. And now you're noticing?"

He gave me a blank stare.

I rolled my eyes. I couldn't believe he was that clueless about how pissed off I was. Not one word had I uttered when he shoved me into his SUV. Shit, even the pack knew I was angry. And smartly, they'd decided to ride in a separate vehicle, trying to stay out of the line of fire.

"I'm going to be clear so we don't have these communication gaps again. I don't like you-woman-me-man caveman shit. Now, I'm not asking you to get all poetic while communicating with me, but I—"

He scoffed. "Good, because that shit ain't happening."

I blew out. *Patience, Light.*

My gorgeous, savage beast was going to take more work than I'd envisioned, but I was up for the job.

"Like I was saying before I was rudely interrupted . . ." I pursed my lips. "I don't expect you to be poetic. Shit, you're incapable of not grunting every other word."

He grunted. I shook my head with dismay.

"But I do expect you not to bark orders at me. I'm your mate, your equal, and I expect to be treated as such. Now, I'm capable of being reasonable, contrary to your belief."

He snorted. I scowled.

"So if you think I'm in fucking danger, communicate with me in a way that won't make me want to punch you in the fucking throat."

The vein along his jaw pulsed. "Do you even get that I'm worried about the Shadows? That I think they're planning another move on you?" He paused. "I won't survive losing you." He glanced at me with pained eyes. "So if you're expecting me to apologize for wanting to protect you, that shit ain't happening."

I sighed, grabbing his hand and kissing his fingers. "I get it. You don't have to be so fucking abrasive about it. That's all I'm saying, alpha."

"I'll work on my delivery." He winked at me. "But I still need those valuable etiquette lessons you promised to give me under the guidance of your mouth on my cock."

I smiled, looking out the driver's window, when the comeback died on my lips as a black SUV slammed into the driver's door, sending us spinning around. My head cracked against the window. Dazed, I pressed a hand to my forehead. My fingers trembled when I felt the bleeding gash.

"Light? You okay?"

My head was pounding as I tried not to give in to the wave of dizziness. "Yes. But we need . . ." My heart stopped when I turned to see his legs crushed under the dashboard, his body pinned by twisted metal. "God! Ryker! I need to get you out," I cried with a panic-filled voice.

Gunfire erupted outside the car. My eyes widened at the sight of masked men firing at Jackal, Rip, and Soar.

Ryker's eyes clouded over with concern. "Light, listen to me. It's too late. They're going to take you."

I yanked unsuccessfully on his seat belt. "No. I can help you get out."

"Light, look at me." His sea-green eyes narrowed. "No matter what happens to me, don't give up. Somehow, I'll find you." He hissed in pain. "Now go!"

I hesitated.

"Light, go!"

My pulse raced as I managed to get out, taking cover between the cars. The masked men continued to shoot. I tried to calm myself. My eyes darted around, looking for the quickest route to safety. My body stiffened, sensing something was wrong, before a man grabbed me, muffling my screams. Two other men helped drag me away as I struggled.

That was the last thing I remembered before everything faded to black.

I KNEW SOMETHING WAS ALL WRONG EVEN BEFORE I OPENED my eyes. I parted my eyelids to see a bunch of men with guns standing around an ornate room. And they weren't speaking

English. I could pick out certain words . . . in French. They were speaking French.

I tried to sit up but collapsed back against the couch. My head was throbbing, and raising my hand to touch my head, I felt the big knot. Motherfuckers had knocked me out.

My gaze was unfocused. I swallowed hard, fearing I had a concussion. Bile rushed up my throat as I gritted my teeth, pushing up on the couch. The men started talking rapidly. The room's door opened. My lips parted. An older man, thin and tall with gray hair, stepped through, with Celina trailing after him.

"Celina?" I blinked. Now I was hallucinating. *Exactly how hard did they hit me?*

Celina's hazel eyes were cold as ice. "Hello, Light."

My eyes widened. "Celina? You're alive?"

Celina smiled, moving toward me, as she raised her arms in the air, seeming drunk with power. "Surprise."

"How . . . how did—what's going on?" I struggled to get on my feet, wobbling forward. I was disoriented.

The older man stepped forward, steadying me.

He angrily looked at Celina. "What part of *do not hurt her* did you not understand?"

Celina rebelliously looked at him. "I did what was necessary."

I pulled my arm away from his grip. "What the fuck do you want?"

I scanned the room, calculating how far I could get before they caught me. Not far. The armed guards blocked the only exit. My eyes darted to the glass interrogation room tucked into the corner. *Shit!* That wouldn't work either.

The man smiled like he'd won the lottery. "You can't escape, Light, but I applaud your spirit."

I stuck up my middle finger. "Applaud this, motherfucker."

He frowned. "You're as rebellious as your mother." He cruelly looked at me. "But I'll break that right out of you . . . with enough time."

I stared at him. "Like hell you will. Who are you?"

"I'm Baptiste Thomas." He shrugged, as if that explained everything.

I swayed but caught myself.

"Are you all right?" He reached for me with a weird look in his eyes.

I widened my stance, preparing to fight my way out. "Don't come near me." I swallowed the bile that threatened to choke me. "If you're going to kill me, prepare for a fight."

Baptiste smiled icily. "If I wanted you dead, you'd be dead already."

Celina stepped forward with a manic look in her eyes. "Baptiste, I brought her to you, like you wanted. Now let's kill her together, like you promised."

"Kill her?" Baptiste reached to caress my cheek.

I swatted his hand away.

"Why would I kill my only granddaughter?"

Celina's eyes narrowed. "What?" she screeched.

He ignored her, looking at me with awe. "I've been waiting years for this moment, Light."

I incredulously looked at him. "Let me get this straight. First you sent men to kidnap me, and then you practically killed me in a car crash. And you want me to smile and embrace you like a damn messiah?"

Celina paced back and forth, pulling at her hair like she was in her own private hell. "No. No. No. You said we would kill her and her whole fucking family."

He coldly looked at her. "I lied."

Celina stopped, her body tight, as she absently clenched her fists. "But you love me. We're going to rule the Others together. You need me."

Baptiste laughed. "Need? I don't need you, and I most certainly don't love you." He grabbed the back of her head, giving her a long, sultry kiss. "God, I'm going to miss your talented and enthusiastic blow jobs." He snapped his fingers, and a guard swiftly moved forward. "Kill her."

Celina squeaked, stepping back. "What? No. I love you. I stole their stupid fucking client list. I betrayed the Credences. I did it all for you." She looked at him with panicked eyes. "I thought that's what you wanted."

He sneered, "That's what you get for thinking."

Celina's eyes darted around, looking for an exit. "Please. We're good together."

Baptiste scoffed. "You were a good fuck, but I would never spend my life with a wolf-shifter."

Celina growled, "No. It's all her fault. It's always about those fucking Credence women. They killed my brother and threw his body into the river like he was trash. They can't get away with it."

She ran toward me with rage-filled eyes. The guard snatched her back, and I watched in horror as she lost a chunk of her hair. She screamed in pain, backing up.

Baptiste laughed. "Well, that's one thing you got wrong, Celina. I killed your brother, Nolan. Just like I'm going to kill you."

"You told me the Credences killed him."

He shrugged. "I lied. How else would I have gotten you to help me? On your knees. Right now." He didn't wait for her to comply. Pushing on the back of her legs, he sent her to the ground, hard.

I was still trying to understand. "Nolan?" I couldn't believe what was happening. I was silent, trying to work through what I was about to see.

A guard moved behind Celina, aiming his gun, flexing to pull the trigger. Shots rang out. Celina fell forward, dead.

"Wha—" I was shaken, both physically and psychologically, trying to process everything that had happened in the last five minutes. I looked at Celina's body sprawled out on the ground. I tried to catch my breath and compose myself.

"You're a fucking psycho." I nervously licked my lips. "Why am I here?"

He nodded to the monitors lining the walls, and Ryker's profile popped up with information about him.

"Why are you doing this?" I pleaded.

He smiled condescendingly. "To protect your ancestors' legacy and you."

My nostrils flared. "So by killing innocent people, you think it justifies your mission?"

He didn't say anything.

I kept going. "You've killed humans and Others. What's next?" My body tensed.

He shrugged. "Destroy the Others. This is what they would have wanted."

My lips flattened. "You are a nut. And I'm out of here." I turned to leave.

The guards aimed their guns at me.

He clasped his hands behind his back. "It will never be that easy, Light. You leave, you die. It's simple."

His phone rang. He pulled it out, looking at the display before giving me a bone-chilling smile. "It's for you."

"How is it for me? No one I know would be calling you."

He arched a brow. "It's the dog you mated."

The fact that he knew about Ryker caught my attention.

"You should let him know you're safe." He handed me the phone.

Confused, I did as instructed. I cleared my throat before answering, "Ryker?"

"Are you okay?" Ryker's voice was tinged with desperation.

My eyes darted to Baptiste. "As okay as I can be."

"Put me on speaker," Ryker demanded.

My fingers fumbled when I pressed the button.

"Baptiste, I know who you are and what you want, and if you touch one hair on her head, I. Will. Kill. You," Ryker retorted in a cold, deadly voice that sent chills through my body.

"I'm afraid not, Mr. Alfero. I am the one holding her. And if you value her life, you will stop the peace treaty negotiations."

Ryker growled. "This has nothing to do with the peace treaty. You want to use Light to create a new race of fae."

Baptiste laughed. "Ah, I see you've found the mole in your pack. I knew Bones was the weakest link. No matter. He served his purpose when he gave us intel on your meeting with Oskar Orlov."

My mouth dropped open. First Noah and now Bones. *How many people have the Shadows corrupted?*

Baptiste continued. "So tell me. When you were done torturing him, did you bury him in the backyard like the dog he was?"

I hissed, my eyes snapping to him. He was a rude fuck who needed to be taught some manners.

"I swear, if you don't let her go . . ." Ryker barked.

Baptiste prowled over to me, snatching the phone from my hand. "Let's cut to the chase, shall we? I will kill her if you don't walk away from the treaty and her."

"So I do both, or you'll kill her? You're a sorry sack of shit."

"What can I say? I'm greedy. And I'm not releasing my beautiful granddaughter." He looked at me with a sick possessive stare, making my stomach turn. "My family has been waiting centuries for Light, and I have no intention of ever letting her go, except in a body bag."

"You sick bastard. You would never kill her. You need her too much," Ryker hissed.

Baptiste ran a hand over my hair. I pushed him away with a snarl.

"My family and the Shadows have killed many people to get what we want. And we're willing to make more sacrifices, starting with her."

"And the end game?" Ryker barked.

"Don't be coy, shifter. You know what we want—the annihilation of all Others." He smiled at me. "And the creation of a new race." He paused. "Now, I know about your little plan to rescue her, and if I were you, I'd rethink it. If I even smell a wolf-shifter anywhere near my compound, I will put a bullet in her brain." He finished before hanging up.

I couldn't hide my shock and damn confusion. "Did you just threaten to kill me?"

His eyes narrowed into cold slits. "And never doubt that I would. I know what's at stake—a new beginning. And despite my followers' beliefs that you're simply not ready, I know you are." He smiled. "I know what kind of asset you can be." He moved past me. "The powers you have can change our world, creating warriors with untold powers."

My eyes widened. "So you think I'm going to breed a race of warriors like some animal?"

He laughed. "This has absolutely nothing to do with sex. You are precious. And when you come into your powers, you will be able to share your gifts with the Shadows, breeding a new race of warriors."

"Do you really think it will be that easy? The Others will hunt you down and kill you."

"We are strong." He smiled arrogantly. "There have been Shadows in existence before you and I were born, and they'll be around when we're dust in the ground. This time, we will win, and all Others will bow at my feet."

"What makes you think I will help you?"

He touched my cheek. "Because I will kill everyone you love if you don't." He sighed tiredly. "I'm also smart enough to know Ryker will keep pursuing the treaty and you, no matter what I say." He shrugged. "It's his nature. But you need to know this story will end badly if he does."

I tried to process this without bawling like a baby. "Well . . . that's . . ."

He gestured to the monitors displaying all of Ryker's and my family's information. "You cooperate with me, and they live. It's simple."

My heart raced. "So the deal is I live as your prisoner for the rest of my life, or my family and mate die?"

"Yes. And if you even think of escaping, I'll kill them, one by one, for fun." He paused, expectantly looking at me. "What's your answer?"

I was resigned at this point and knew I was fighting an uphill battle. I looked over at the monitors.

He got no answer, so he grabbed the remote, shutting off the monitors. "You have a little bit of time to think about it, Light."

I stepped forward. "I'll do anything for my family and mate. But know that you're playing with dynamite. Be careful it doesn't blow up in your face, Thomas."

He smiled like the Cheshire Cat. "Good. Now we leave." He snapped his fingers at the armed guards. "Sanitize this place from top to bottom. We don't need the shifters finding any intel." He pointed to the interrogation room. "Start there first."

At that moment, something exploded outside the door. The blast shook the walls and floor.

"Go, you idiots!" he snarled at his guards before snatching me by the neck, a gun pointed at my head.

The guards rallied in front of the door with guns drawn.

❧ 23 ☙

RYKER

I nodded to Soar. "Do it."

We moved back as Soar set the explosive. The room's door blasted open. Jackal, Rip, and Soar barreled into the room, raining gunfire on the guards, mowing them down. I strode into the room with my gun drawn. I stopped when I saw the terrified look on Light's face as Baptiste held a gun to her throat.

"You shoot, she dies! Everyone, back up now!" Baptiste said coldly.

"How are you, darling?" I moved, keeping my gun out of sight.

Light shrugged. "Peachy. As you can tell, this family reunion is absolutely fabulous."

Baptiste started dragging Light over to the door of a glass-walled interrogation room. The fear I smelled wafting off Light's body sent my beast into panic mode. I pushed down the beast fighting me for control and the right to protect Light.

I lurched forward, watching as Light fought Baptiste all the way over to the interrogation room.

"No! God, Baptiste. Let me go. No! Let me go. Please!" she pleaded.

I raised my gun, aiming at Baptiste's head, but I didn't have a clear shot. "Don't! Don't do it!" I barked at Baptiste.

Baptiste pressed the gun into Light's neck. "Before you let off one round, she'll be dead. Back up now!"

He slammed his hand against a biometric pad to open the door and then backed in. The door slid shut, and Baptiste stood in front of the glass, staring at me with a smug smile.

I turned to Rip, my weapons and technology expert. "Open that fucking door!"

"On it." Rip pulled off the cover on the biometric pad.

I dropped the gun to my side. I knew, without a doubt, that the glass was bulletproof. My fists tightened. "I love you, Light," I hissed with emotions choking me.

The tiniest smile passed over her mouth as she realized what I'd said. My heart jumped when I saw tears trailing down her cheeks. My eyes narrowed as the glass turned opaque. I could no longer see Baptiste and Light.

"What the fuck did you do, Rip?" I barked.

"Nothing. That's not me. Baptiste did it," he grunted. "Stand back. I'm in."

We all waited, surrounding the door with guns drawn, and it slid open.

I stared in shock. The room was empty. "Search the room for any hidden exits."

My pack fanned out, thoroughly searching the room.

They all said in unison, "Nothing."

I stood with my hands clenched. "I will find you, Light, and Baptiste will die. This I promise."

~

THANK YOU FOR READING **WHEN LIGHTNING STRIKES!**

More Credence Curse Series goodness continues with **TAMING THE BEAST!**

She refuses to love. He'll stop at nothing to have her. Together, can they fulfill their deepest desires?

GET A FREE SEDONA VENEZ BOOK!

https://sedonavenez.com/free-book

WANT FREE SEDONA VENEZ BOOKS?

Sign up for Sedona Venez's Newsletter and receive FREE BOOKS. In addition to the free stories, you will also get special pricing, exclusive previews and news of new releases.

GET A FREE SEDONA VENEZ BOOK!

Join Sedona's mailing list to be the first to know of new releases, free books, special prices and other author giveaways.

https://sedonavenez.com/free-book

OTHER TITLES BY SEDONA VENEZ

SciFi Romance
Galaxy Alien Warriors - The Box Set
Beauty and the Alien Beast

Paranormal Romance
Shifter Alphas Furever Series
Claimed by Her Two Alphas
Claimed by Her Wolf
Claimed by Her Bear
Claimed by Her Dragon

Paranormal Romance
Credence Curse Series
When Lightning Strikes
Taming the Beast
Reason to Love

Wolf Shifter Romance
Wolf Elite Series
Operation Wolf: Gunner
Operation Wolf: Eli

Operation Wolf: Hunter

Bears Shifter Romance
Bear Elite Series
Bear's Mission

Enemies-to-Lovers Romance
Dirty Secrets Series
Twisted Lies
Twisted Lies 2
Twisted Lies 3
Twisted Lies 4

Friends-to-Lovers Romance
Heart of Fire

MFM Ménage Romance
Standalone
Shameless Desires

Billionaire Boss Romance
Standalone
Mr. Billionaire CEO

Urban Fantasy Romance
Magic Fire Collection

ABOUT THE AUTHOR

USA TODAY BESTSELLING AUTHOR SEDONA VENEZ lives in New York City with her hot ex-military hubby—hooah—and their fur babies. She loves writing sizzling, sexy intricate stories about strong but broken characters who push limits, overcome their fears and risk it all for love.

Sedona loves to connect with readers!
www.sedonavenez.com

www.ingramcontent.com/pod-product-compliance
Lightning Source LLC
Chambersburg PA
CBHW070943180726
48291CB00004B/1117